MAESTRO OF DESTRUCTION

Bam-Bam-Bam!

Whatever was going on in there, those were the musical notes being played by the winners. Beeker understood the ways these symphonies of death were performed. He only wished that he was sure who the composer was.

Suddenly there was silence.

Appelbaum was swinging his M-60 back and forth on its bipod, just waiting for someone to show his head and give him another excuse to play his deadly song. But there was nothing at all. Fear wasn't something he was used to feeling, but the sweat gathered on Beeker's forehead. He wondered if this silence was the sign that someone in there was getting ready for the final and most complete suicidal act of all—the detonation of the atomic bombs that would remove all trace of them from the face of the earth!

CONTRACT: TERROR SUMMIT

BOOKS BY MICHAEL MCDOWELL AND JOHN PRESTON

THE BLACK BERETS

Deadly Reunion

Cold Vengeance

The Black Palm

Contract: White Lady

Louisiana Firestorm

The Death Machine Contract

The Red Man Contract

D.C. Death March

The Night of the Jaguar

Contract: Terror Summit

The Samurai Contract

The Akbar Contract

Blue Water Contract

CONTRACT: TERROR SUMMIT

MICHAEL MCDOWELL & JOHN PRESTON

BLACK STONE PUBLISHING

ISBN 979-8-200-88208-3
Fiction / War & Military

Version 1

Blackstone Publishing
31 Mistletoe Rd.
Ashland, OR 97520

www.BlackstonePublishing.com

For A. E. Coffin
Some of the best Marine Corps material I ever met

1

Cowboy did not like this one bit. Not one damn bit. Someplace out there in the Sahara there were five big bombs. The Black Berets were being sent to get them. There was one for each of them. If the five men didn't accomplish that little task, the world wouldn't have to worry about much more. There probably wouldn't be much of a world left.

The mission they were on was one of the most crucial they'd ever attempted. But the possibility of renegade nuclear devices wasn't what was getting to Cowboy. He had something much more immediate to deal with. There was an element to this operation that was even more agitating.

Someone else was flying the goddamn airplane!

His stomach was churning from the roller-coaster effect of the Bronco's rough ride. The idiot pilot wasn't competent, that was all there was to it.

Of course—as far as he was concerned—no pilot but himself could possibly have gotten this or any other aircraft up off the ground, let alone be able to fly it underneath the Libyan radar.

This was a special kind of flying. It called for a skill that he was *sure* he and he alone had mastered. You had to take the plane and, in the middle of the night, using the most sophisticated instruments possible, fly only a hundred feet above the ground. At the most. Anything more and you were gone. The blip on the radar would be big and loud and all of a sudden you'd have a whole squadron of Soviet-built MIGs on your ass and it would be all over.

Cowboy had done it often. He'd done it in Nam and he'd done it in the United States when he was taking his little vacation that just happened to be financed by a very large drug-smuggling operation. He knew *he* could fly a plane so close to the ground that the belly would touch the top of a cactus. He knew it because he'd done it to get away from the Coast Guard and the Border Patrol on so many occasions he couldn't count them all.

That didn't mean that the joker at the controls of this thing could do it.

The plane suddenly jerked up. Cowboy swore that half his stomach was left on the floor of the plane. He was going to puke. That was all there was to it. He was going to lose his cookies and goddamn the rest of them if they insisted on letting some asshole who probably didn't know the first thing about planes . . .

He felt Rosie behind him. The big black man's stomach was rumbling. *Don't you dare do that on me*, Cowboy warned silently. He didn't bother speaking out loud because the roar of the Bronco's engines would have drowned him out in any event. That was another thing. It added insult to injury that they were flying into goddamn Libyan territory on a shit-eating Bronco, for Christ's sake.

The Bronco had been one of the workhorses of the American forces in Nam. But it had been beneath the dignity of a pilot like Cowboy to take the controls of one of the things.

He had flown almost everything else—copters, jet interceptors, you name it. But the Bronco was strictly bush league. The main purpose of the plane had been to transport matériel to the front. But they were too slow and they were too cumbersome to be exciting. Cowboy had gone only for the excitement.

That's how he got here, sitting with his legs around a damn Greek monster with a black monster's huge feet straddling his own waist in the back of the plane. At least the bulky parachutes they were wearing kept them from having to get too close to one another. Thank God for small miracles, that's all Cowboy would say. It was bad enough to almost be sitting in Rosie's lap.

For the second time in the last fifteen minutes, Cowboy damned the day that he'd ever met Billy Leaps Beeker. The Indian was no good, that's all there was to it. It was bad enough that he'd gotten Cowboy into the Black Berets; it was inexcusable that Beeker had let someone else take the controls of this fucking airplane!

The plane took a sudden lurch downward, and there was Cowboy's stomach on the ceiling. There was no doubt that he was going to puke. None. His stomach couldn't take the torture.

They were lined up with their legs wrapped around one another in preparation for a night drop into the middle of the Libyan Desert. It was the kind of maneuver that was simply part of war for a soldier.

They might be the best little private army in the world and they might be the richest mercenaries on the face of the globe, but they were still soldiers and they still had to go on missions. Missions meant danger. This particular mission meant they were dropping from the sky. All of that Cowboy could understand. He could accept it all. But he could not accept the fact that he wasn't at the controls of the damn plane.

Cowboy had been flying since he was barely adolescent. His daddy had been a barnstormer while he was growing up. Cowboy had a secret suspicion that good old dad and mom had even conceived him during one of their crop-dusting runs. It would make sense.

He'd learned how to fly as easily as other men learn how to ride a bike. Then, one day, he'd gone to an air show with his father and had seen some huge jet fighters. The prop planes he'd been playing with had been great, but they'd been nothing compared to the huge metal birds.

It turned out that jet planes were a bit more complicated than crop dusters. If you wanted to get behind the controls of one of the big monsters, they told him, you have to go to college. It seemed like a decent price to pay to learn how to fly faster than the speed of sound. Cowboy, who hadn't really given a second's thought to his future before the day at the air show, suddenly was desperately interested in attending Texas A&M University.

He'd gone and excelled, picking up more than a fair amount of computer knowledge along the way. He wasn't really interested in the new machines, but they'd told him that he had to understand them if he was going to fly the next generation of jets. That sold him. He was determined that he would fly anything they made. He had just about done that so far and there wasn't any indication that Boeing or Lockheed or anyone else was going to break his record.

God knows the world seemed to try when they sent him to Nam. He'd been the star attraction in that huge target practice. It made no difference what kind of jet or which model helicopter he flew, they still shot missiles and bullets and God only knows what else at him.

Nam was where he'd met up with this gang of jokers who were crowded into the rear of the Bronco in full gear waiting to jump into the Libyan night and show the world that they were mean enough and tough enough to take on Qadhafi and anyone else who got in their way.

It had all started with Beeker. It was the same for all of them. They'd been just joes in Nam. Each of them a little special, but not so extraordinary that he'd stood out in the crowd, really. But the half-breed Cherokee had made the rounds, asked the right people the right questions, and then he'd assembled them all in one place and told them they had a new name: They were the Black Berets.

They fought together, loved women together, drank together, they did everything. They'd become family, brothers joined by the blood of the hundreds of enemies they'd met on the field. Nam had been a question of survival. Beeker had decided they were going to survive, it was that simple.

And they had.

The only problem was that when the war was over and they had separated, the life they'd led in Southeast Asia had ruined them. It had taken away Cowboy's real name, for one thing. He still couldn't quite remember how to spell Sherwood Hatcher when it came time for him to fill out a passport application or some other official document. He'd *become* Cowboy by then.

That name change was just one more symbol of how much the Black Berets had taken over his life. He'd moved back to the States and, in his native Texas, he'd joined up with some awfully interesting businessmen who were very, very pleased to discover someone who could fly just about any airplane they happened to put on the tarmac.

They were especially pleased that this man named Cowboy didn't seem to mind if the flight plans they gave him happened to include some stops in exotic places like Peru and Colombia. Nor did he protest when they asked if he couldn't find a way to deliver the imported goods that would allow them to avoid the unpleasantness of the U.S. Customs office. The bureaucracy was such a bother.

Since his pay had included very full and very pure packages of white powder that helped him to keep his nasal passages clear, Cowboy had been very willing to accommodate these easy requests. He'd been very willing indeed.

Cowboy was actually lucky that he had lost only his name in Vietnam. There had been other things that happened to him over there. Any man who came out of the stinking war had memories of the innocence that he'd lost in the jungles. At least Cowboy had a cloud of cocaine to let him gloss over the rest of the agony that came from being back in the States. The rest of the Black Berets hadn't been so fortunate.

They'd tried to meld into American civilian society, they honestly had tried as much as they could. But it hadn't worked at all. The big black man behind Cowboy was one example of that.

Roosevelt Boone—just Rosie to his friends—had discovered that the only skill that he'd brought back from Nam was his inability to be grossed out by human death or injury. There was nothing that had to do with human destruction that could affect him anymore.

The big burn clinic at Newark General Hospital found a way to make that strange aspect of Rosie's personality useful. They put him in a room in the basement and gave him some fancy surgical-steel implements and set him to work peeling the skin off of cadavers. Human skin was the only thing that could help some burn victims. A violent city like Newark had an awesome hunger for more and more of it.

The cold bodies would be wheeled into Rosie's private sanctum and he'd go to work, whistling the whole time. He'd freaked more than a few of the people with his habit of talking to the dead bodies, telling them of the good they would be doing for the living, easing their pain and helping to cure them.

That was the best Rosie could do—or at least it was the

best that a peacetime society could do with Rosie. That is, it was the best until Beeker went and brought him back to the Black Berets. He'd reclaimed Rosie's life and made him put a uniform back on. He'd put a rifle in Rosie's hands again and he'd told him that his soul belonged to the small corps of men that sat in this very Bronco as it continued its roller-coaster way over the sandy terrain of North Africa.

Rosie wasn't the only one that Beeker had gotten.

There'd been the Greek man sitting in front of Cowboy right now. If Cowboy had trouble remembering how to spell his own legal name, he couldn't begin to get through Harry's. It was Haralambos Georgeos Pappathanassiou.

Harry had come back to the United States more wounded than the rest of them. But his wounds weren't the physical kind that you could see, and you certainly couldn't heal them. Harry's wounds were inside, deep inside. They showed only in the air of intense melancholy that the huge, muscled man displayed in a mien of constant sadness.

Harry seemed to carry the sorrows of the world on his shoulders. He had gone through a lot. Cowboy knew about most of it. When he'd returned Stateside, Harry had gone back to Chicago and he'd reopened his family bar in a working-class neighborhood. He spent his days there listening to the meaningless complaints of the customers. He clenched up at night and then, after they'd all left, he'd take his bottle of cheap scotch to bed with him and down it in straight shots. Harry had always hoped—though it seldom worked—that the booze would let him sleep with just a little peace and relief from his memories.

Then Beeker'd come and all he had to say was, "We're going back."

They'd all thought that "going back" meant they were just on their way to Southeast Asia again. Beeker probably thought that too. They did make it into Laos on a wild-goose chase after rumors of living MIAs. But it had been a scam that someone had run on them. There was no one there when they'd arrived.

But the very fact of having regrouped and having been able to feel once more what it was like to be a part of the team had been too strong a narcotic. They had gone back—but back to something even stronger than the memories of Vietnam. They had gone back to being Black Berets. There was no way they could give it up after they'd tasted a drug stronger than Cowboy's coke and a booze more addictive than Harry's scotch.

They were the Black Berets.

Even Marty. The memory of the little runt was cause for another attack of nausea. Marty Appelbaum was a skinny, blond-haired, asthmatic Jew from New Jersey whose personality had absolutely no justification for existence—except he liked bombs. Marty loved explosives of every kind. Cowboy figured that most people like Marty had spent their childhoods tearing the wings off innocent insects.

Marty had been a little different at least. He'd spent his years as a boy figuring out how to put enough match heads together to blow the lock off his mother's closet door.

He'd seen a documentary once about underwater demolitions that had created an almost orgasmic response in his puny little frame. The idea that there was a place where you could set off an incendiary device and not have to worry about minor problems like fire wardens and such was such heaven to the small man that he'd held to the fantasy of joining the Navy with a passion more intense than any other of his life. As soon as he was old enough, Marty signed up.

Marty had become a SEAL, one of the elite force that the Navy used in the war to patrol the rivers of the Mekong Delta and to make sure the harbors of Vietnamese ports were free from any interference. He'd been able to blow up bridges, destroy enemy craft, do a whole list of things that had been only vague dreams in his hyperactive mind until he'd found the war. And then he'd found Beeker and the Black Berets.

The rest of them hadn't wanted Marty to be part of the team when Beeker had called them all back together. But they had to let him in. They had to because of his awesome skills. Marty had even found a way to use his specialty in peacetime society.

He'd been in St. Louis, one of the dying cities of the Midwest. Marty had discovered the art of implosion. He could place explosives in the shell of old buildings and detonate them in such a way that the structure would fall in on itself and not destroy other more valuable property or people.

But that hadn't been a true love for him. It had been too tame. It had limited his ability to *create*. Marty liked to call himself the Michelangelo of mayhem. He liked to color coordinate his explosions and he loved being able to set up a carefully synchronized series of eruptions.

The simple act of imploding a building that time had passed by wasn't enough for him. It limited his art to a frame that was too confining. He wanted a large canvas. He wanted the world. And Billy Leaps Beeker was giving it to him.

They had all come back together and, once they had, they knew they couldn't separate again. They were nothing as individuals. They were everything as the Black Berets. Alone, they were simple numbers in the census; as a team, they were a force that the world was beginning to recognize as a fearsome power.

Cowboy's stomach was starting to calm down now. The plane seemed to have found a plateau, and it was skimming the flat surface. He took a deep breath and tried to make himself relax. There might—there just *might*—be another person in the world who was possibly competent enough to pilot a twin-engine plane across a level piece of terrain. He wouldn't want to bet too much money on it, but the possibility was real enough that he had to take it into account.

Cowboy sighed deeply. There were no windows in this part of the Bronco. There was only the blackness and the feel of the other men's bodies and one red light. He couldn't hear them over the drone of the engines. The sound of their breathing might have been a comfort. It could have been a kind of evidence of the existence of the team. He needed that right now.

After all, they were going to jump into the backyard of Qadhafi, the monster of Africa. The one true living evil in the world was down there just waiting for people like the Berets to even attempt to invade his private preserve. It wasn't a pleasant thought to imagine what might be involved in this little adventure.

Sure, they were the Black Berets, but they were also just five men: Cowboy, Rosie, Harry, and Marty—but of course there was also Beeker, and that was the one thing that made all the difference.

As the cold, black Saharan night sped past outside the metal walls of the Bronco, Cowboy thought about the leader of the Berets.

William Leaps Beeker, Jr. The son of a Marine, the son of a bitch who was a Marine. Beeker was a half-breed who'd grown up on an Oklahoma reservation ignoring the destitute poverty that was all around him and waiting, just waiting, for the day he could join the Corps. His father had died on some hill in Korea that was so insignificant that it didn't even have a name, just a number. But that didn't mean anything to Beeker. His father had died a warrior's honorable death.

The goddamn Cherokee had lied his underaged way into boot camp. He hadn't just survived Parris Island, he'd gloried in it. He came out with gung ho tattooed on his heart, so deep inside him that you didn't have to see the words on his skin. You could hear their echoes whenever he walked within ten feet of you. He had been the one the brass had chosen to put together the Black Berets in Nam. They owed it all to him.

All of it—the good and the bad.

Cowboy had first come across Beeker when the Marine had told him that he couldn't take off from an LZ in the middle of a firefight. There were still some wounded leathernecks who had to be picked up. Every rule in the book said that the pilot was supposed to get the hell out of there. His training and the expense of the aircraft were worth more to Saigon than a platoon of ignorant jarheads. But there had been something so convincing about the well-muscled and intense half-breed sergeant that the pilot had stayed much longer than he had to.

A lot of it had to do with the calm but convincing way Beeker had told him that he'd protect the copter. Why should Cowboy have believed that one single Marine could do what so many others hadn't been able to? He never did figure out where that blind trust had come from. He only knew that it had worked.

There'd been a dozen other occasions when Beeker had calmly told the pilot to do something that defied reason, when he'd convinced Cowboy to take one more chance that might give another Marine an opportunity to escape from Charlie, or else one more flyover to give Beeker a shot at taking out an enemy encampment.

Cowboy had accumulated a trophy case full of medals, thanks to Beeker. He didn't have a single use for any one of them. But they were the symbol of his attachment to the bastard. They might as well be wedding rings.

A second red light went on at the back of the plane. This was the first signal. They were approaching their DZ, the drop zone where the LA-LO maneuver was going to take them.

LA-LO was a very simple acronym: Low Altitude-Low Opening. So simple, Cowboy thought to himself, so very . . . It meant just what it said. The Bronco was flying at low altitude. It was going to jump up in the air at the designated moment and then the five Black Berets were all going to slip out the suddenly opened rear end of the plane and they were going to fall a short distance.

His body hurt just thinking about it. The straps that attached him to his parachute were already digging into his legs. When he was rolled out of the plane and his chute automatically opened, the sudden force of the jolt would make the canvas tear into his thighs. It was only a question of a few inches and the frigging things could get his crown jewels.

Cowboy carefully adjusted his genitals in his Jockey shorts to make sure nothing was slipping out and taking a chance of being harmed by the straps. That was something he didn't need to have happen, not at all.

He could sense the rest of them going about the last-minute checks after they had seen the red light go on. They had their packs, their "sterile" weapons. Like their uniforms, there was nothing on them that could identify them as United States troops. They weren't, really. They were strictly freelance these days. But the government had been extra careful to make sure that there was no way they could be tied to Washington if they failed or were captured.

He got ready. He told his stomach to calm down. He knew there was one more really big loop on the roller coaster coming. It was the one that was going to send them tumbling out into space. Then all he'd have to worry about was his chute opening. He clutched on to the shoulder straps of the parachute and waited.

Somehow, he decided, it wouldn't be so bad to be falling

into the sky and being dependent on the huge piece of fabric. At least there wouldn't be any other pilot to worry about. There wouldn't be another human being who could fuck up his life by making the wrong decision . . .

Wait a minute! He suddenly realized that this chute had been packed by some unknown person. Someone who he had never met had put it all together, and how the hell was he supposed to know if that person had known what he was doing? A new panic caught hold of his heart. He wasn't at all sure about this jumping thing anymore. What if . . .

But Cowboy didn't have enough time to let the new concerns percolate into something real. The Bronco suddenly nosed up. Its engines struggled as the pilot forced all the power he could out of them. The men started to slide downward as the plane approached a 90-degree angle. It would appear as a slight aberration on the Libyan radar screen, that was all. But Cowboy couldn't even think about that. *Green light!* The rear door of the Bronco suddenly opened, and all five of them were sailing out into nothingness. It didn't even matter if their parachutes opened or not. There was no doubt they were going to end up on the floor of the Sahara Desert. The only question was: Would they be alive when they hit the ground?

2

Billy Leaps Beeker quickly dug into the sand with his hands. The other four Black Berets were doing the same thing. There hadn't been any indication that they had been sighted, but they weren't going to leave the evidence of their arrival out in the open for the Libyans or any of their friends to find in the morning.

As soon as he had gotten far enough down into the shifting desert, Beeker took the already-bunched-up parachute and buried it in the hole he'd made. When he was finished, the chute was in four feet of sand. The windblown desert was a constantly shifting terrain. The hiding place might be revealed soon, much sooner than it would have been on more solid ground. But that was a chance they'd have to take. They weren't expecting to be around for a long time in any event.

Beeker stood. He was the first one done. He automatically took a sentry role while the rest of them continued with their tasks.

The automatic rifle he had in his hand felt unfamiliar. He was well trained in its use and there was no question about his ability with it. Still, the Czechoslovakian Vz25 wasn't one of his favorites. It bothered him to carry a ComBloc weapon. But they had to come in without anything on them that could be accurately traced back to the United States.

In addition to the Czech rifle, they also had CZ 83 semiautomatic Czech pistols in their shoulder holsters. The two weapons weren't shabby, that wasn't Beeker's complaint. In fact, the Vz25 had been the machine whose technology made the feared Israeli UZI possible. The CZ 83 was far superior to almost all NATO handguns. With these and the accompanying Czech-made combat knives, they were well armed for this little trip to Mr. Qadhafi's homeland.

It didn't help to know that the Czechs had made decent products. It wasn't a source of consolation that they did a far better job at creating the tools of war than they did in filling up the shops for their nation's housewives. Beeker knew that he wasn't the only one who would have preferred an American-made arsenal for this trip.

The desert night was surprisingly cool. The breezes that swept over the barren desert had a hint of the Mediterranean in them. They were a long way from the shore, but the stereotype of the blistering wasteland wasn't evident here.

Beeker squatted down on the ground. He took a map out of the inside of his uniform shirt. He knew that in a few hours, when the sun had come up and turned the sand into a reflecting oven, he'd regret having even that light covering. But now the cotton fabric felt awfully good.

He used his Vz25 to hold down one side of the chart. His hand secured the other. He flipped on the flashlight clipped to his combat harness. He felt Cowboy crouching beside him before he actually looked up and saw the pilot studying the marks with him.

Then Rosie came over, and he also was plotting their precise location. In a few minutes all of the other Berets had finished hiding their parachutes and were gathered around their leader waiting for the next stage of the operation to begin.

"We're only a few miles from where al-Kaldi is supposed to have his headquarters. Intelligence says there are at least fifty well-armed men in his camp. There's a contingent of trainees in there with them. They've come to learn the latest tricks in the terrorist trade. If we're lucky, the training exercises will be the most important thing going on and there won't be heavy security.

"We have to get into the heart of the camp and find out if they have the goods. If they do, we have to get them out."

They'd been over it all a hundred times. But that didn't mean that they were upset that their leader would repeat the whole thing once more. They knew that when you went on an assignment like this one, you had to have every tiny detail nailed down—or else you'd be nailed yourself.

They all nodded their agreement and Beeker stood up, folding the map back up again and shoving it inside his clothing. He took the Vz25 and put it over his shoulder along with the extra-heavy backpack they each had to carry for Marty. Then he began to lead them toward the camp of al-Kaldi and—he hoped with all the passion he had at his command—the stolen goods that were threatening the very existence of the world.

The word to go to Libya had come from Delilah. Most of their operations started with one of her messages. As he trudged along the loose soil of the desert, Beeker thought about the strange and beautiful woman.

In another world he'd usually be happy to hear from the blonde. She was, after all, probably the most beautiful woman he knew. And he'd known plenty of them. She had a body that went right to the limits of pornographic male fantasies of what a female should be. Her breasts were larger than life, her hips firmer than dreams. But it was probably her smell—some hard-to-define combination of perfume and female musk—that got to him the most.

Just the idea of her flashing through his mind right now was creating a serious distraction. He tried to wipe her out of his consciousness. But she wouldn't go. It wasn't just that her sexuality was so powerful, it was also the simple reality that she was the messenger.

She'd shown up at the ranch in Louisiana, unannounced as usual. She just walked into his life the way she liked to do and smiled the way he liked. She told him there was something he had to do. He had looked at her and he'd tried to dismiss her entreaties—once again. He never could accept the fact that it would never work.

She talked to him using all the skills she'd developed in the past years they'd been together. She played on his patriotism, she pulled out all the stops in appealing to his responsibilities and his commitments. There was something terrible going on and he had to use his team to help the world.

It was never to help the neighborhood. God forbid he could be called upon only to give a friend a hand with getting in his crops or lending him a bit of money. Not with Delilah. With her it was always Billy Leaps Beeker saving the goddamn world.

There was a sudden break in the blackness of night as the team of five men kept up their journey. Dawn was just beginning to approach. As soon as the sun came up Beeker would feel the temperature starting to rise. The respite from the cruel Saharan day was going to be over soon.

Delilah . . . He tried to keep his mind from going back to her, but the closer they got to al-Kaldi's camp, the more she intruded.

She'd obviously gotten her way. He refused to think that either one of them were so shallow that the times they spent in bed had anything to do with his decisions. He'd come for other, higher reasons. Because, in the end, she found the one button that pushed something deep inside him—it always did.

The boy.

It was a simple thing that she had said to Beeker. You have to go to Africa and you have to take out al-Kaldi because, if you don't, he might start a nuclear war and, if he does, there won't be anything left for Tsali or any of the children.

The seventeen-year-old full-blooded Cherokee was the most precious thing on earth to Beeker. Billy Leaps had married a couple of times. They'd been bad mistakes he'd made, unrealistic attempts to fit in with mainstream America. He regretted those marriages and the time they had wasted. He was furious whenever he realized that they hadn't produced the one thing that he wanted more than anything else in the world—a son.

He had the team, he had his friends with him, and his work. But he was going through his life without the one thing that any man really wanted. He'd been resigned to that fate. Then while hunting one day he'd come across a pair of redneck idiots who were playing their machismo games with a scrawny Indian boy.

They'd tied him up to a tree and were threatening his life because he'd trespassed on their egos. That was the last time either one of them had a chance to make a protest about the presence of an Indian on the white man's earth. Beeker's .30-.30 had blown them apart. They were buried under the ground now, their flesh turned to the same dust that had made up their hearts.

But they had achieved one thing during their miserable lifetimes. They'd given Beeker his greatest desire. Tsali was a full-blooded Cherokee, a being so rare and precious that it seemed he shouldn't have existed.

Beeker was only a half-breed. His father had married an Anglo woman. The only real proof of that marriage was the blue of Billy Leaps's eyes. But Tsali was pure, unblemished by the erosion of white society and unbent in his pursuit of dignity.

He was mute. Some might have thought that made the boy a cripple. Beeker thought it was just one more symbol of Tsali's innocence that he didn't have to go through life mouthing the empty phrases of other men.

The sun was coming up over the horizon now. It burst forth in a blaze. Even though Beeker had seen it happen many other times, it always amazed him how daylight just happened in the desert. It was as quick as the turn of a light switch. Daylight. And when it came, heat.

He could feel the itchiness as his armpits began to sweat. Beads of perspiration came down his forehead. They were close to their target, thank God. They wouldn't have to suffer much of this. They'd do what they had to and get the fuck out.

They'd do what they had to for Tsali.

The endless games of the Washington bureaucrats meant nothing to Beeker and probably meant less to his men. They had all seen the thousands of ways that federal government policy could cause needless death and suffering when they were in Vietnam. There had been those idiots from CIA headquarters and Army Intelligence and God only knew where else who would sit in their air-conditioned offices in Saigon and tell real, live, breathing men to go to this quadrant, assault that position, reconnoiter that area.

The men were just pawns on some big electronic chessboard that the desk jockeys thought they could move around without ever having to deal with the human elements of pain, loss, injury—or death. It had been the men like the Berets who were their toys.

There was little that Beeker had seen to make him think that Washington had changed. He had refused countless attempts to get him to deploy his seasoned force of Black Berets in other battlegrounds that the officials thought needed their special attention.

God knows they'd tried. They'd lied to the Berets, they'd cajoled Beeker, and they'd even tried to entrap them in a series of misadventures. But the men had turned them away time after time. They'd stayed on their Louisiana farm, playing with the expensive toys they could buy now with the vast amounts of money they'd acquired over the years in the field, and they'd tried to live a decent life.

But it couldn't go on forever. And Delilah had known that one key, the password that would force Billy Leaps to bring them out and into the open.

The world will go up in smoke and there won't be anything left for the boy.

So here they were, in the Sahara, marching through the shifting sands of the desert on their way to one more appointment with history, even if the historians would never write about this one any more than they would about the other things the Black Berets had done since they'd been recomposed into a team.

But at least there'd be a history. Because the Berets were going to make sure that some dumb-assed Palestinian terrorist didn't up the ante on the earth's chances for survival.

3

It had taken only a half hour of sunlight for Harry's uniform to be drenched in sweat. He didn't pay much attention to it. When he'd been twelve years old his body hair had sprouted out, seemingly all at once. He had so much of it that the kids on the block used to tease him about being a bear. With the hirsute coat came sweat. It was just natural. He'd lived with it for years.

He was on his belly looking over a ridge onto the Palestinian camp. There was nothing surprising going on down there. The intelligence reports said some Basque nationalists were visiting al-Kaldi this week. They'd get caught in the fight then. It vaguely registered in Harry's mind that the Basques were probably going to die.

He surveyed the scene and his mind noted the facts in computerlike fashion. There were some metal shacks, modern-day Quonset huts. The sun would bounce off the shiny metallic skins of the buildings and give some relief from the cooking heat of the desert. There didn't seem to be any women around, only males were in sight at least. Harry was pleased about that. Somehow it was difficult to anticipate a battle with women.

He could see the firing range off to the south of the camp. There were men taking target practice there. A small airstrip was empty to the north. It was only for use for small planes that brought people in and out of the supposedly secret encampment.

Harry and the others had wondered how Americans discovered the camp when the Israelis had been searching for it so desperately for months. They, like the rest of the world, were used to the awesome capabilities of the Mossad. It was strange to think that the CIA—or whatever agency Washington had working these days, it was hard to keep up with the federal networks—could get something that the Mossad hadn't. But then the Mossad didn't have as many satellites as the CIA.

Al-Kaldi was the most wanted man in the world as far as the Israelis were concerned. He had been the mastermind of a particularly loathsome attack on innocent Jewish tourists in France six months ago. Responding to some perceived slight by the Palestinian cause, al-Kaldi had a busload of Hebrew students murdered with a land mine. There had been some whose bodies had been blown into such small pieces that their remains had never been identified.

The Mossad had pulled out all the stops. They'd even gone so far as to have the Israeli Air Force intercept some Arab commercial airlines and force them to land in Tel Aviv. But it hadn't worked. There were hints—and these weren't the only ones—that the Mossad wasn't as omnipotent as people had once believed.

Harry wondered if—when they were finished with this camp—they couldn't leave some misleading evidence to make others suspect that the Mossad had actually carried out the mission.

The one thing the Black Berets didn't want was more publicity. They'd already gotten too much word-of-mouth talk going about themselves in the mercenary underground. There was nothing to be gained by it. They didn't want more assignments. They didn't want notoriety. They just wanted to be left alone in Louisiana. All you got from a big reputation was big enemies.

Harry ran the back of his hand over his forehead to wipe away an accumulation of sweat. He'd just taken another drink and another salt tablet, a little bit of defense against the possibility of becoming dehydrated here in the desert. That was one of the worst kinds of death, because you just slipped into a state something like unconsciousness. You started to believe things that weren't true and see things that weren't there and you went slowly mad.

Harry smiled to himself when he thought that. He was already mad. He was already living in a state of suspended reality and constant mental pain. Why else would he be here on his belly in the middle of the Sahara waiting to kill a few dozen people whose names he didn't even know?

He gripped the Vz25 and let it roll a bit in his hand. The rifle was superbly built. Why couldn't the Russians and the Czechs do something this good for their kids and wives? Why did the world have to keep on finding ways to destroy people instead of making them happy? Those were questions that always went through Harry's mind when he was on a mission.

There was some movement down in the camp. He saw a man burst out of one of the metal shacks. There was an entourage of people around him. He was clearly someone important. Harry took the Czech gun and got the man in his telescopic sights. Maybe that was al-Kaldi. If he could eliminate him now, maybe they could just pack up and all go home.

As Harry watched through the sight he realized he was just dreaming. Maybe the sun was getting to him after all. They weren't after the terrorist leader. They were hoping they'd find the bombs on him and stop him—or whoever it was—from using the ultimate terrorist weapon on helpless civilian populations. Getting rid of al-Kaldi wasn't going to solve their problem.

The distance was over 1,000 meters—too far for sharpshooting with this rifle in any event. Harry, like the rest of the Black Berets, was a peerless marksman. But he couldn't remanufacture the Vz25 on the spot. Too bad, he had to pass up the shot.

The rifles had been carefully treated with a matte finish so their metal parts wouldn't give off any reflection in the torturous Saharan sun. That had been the way that many other teams had been discovered—and defeated. They hadn't bothered painting their gun barrels and the unexpected glint of the polished steel had given away their position to the enemy. Harry looked around the horizon to see where the other Berets had been positioned. He couldn't spot them. Good.

Their uniforms weren't the usual ones that the Black Berets wore. That had been a disappointment. Harry and the rest of them had come to think of the act of putting on the handmade outfits that Beeker had made for them as something special. They were like Beeker's ancestors, putting on their totemlike face paintings before going into battle. Not this time. The desert called for a different, lighter-colored camouflage.

Harry realized that he could actually stand up right now and not be seen by the troops down in the small valley in front of him. Maybe they'd make out his dark hair, that would be all. And from a distance that would make him look like one of theirs. His Greek features were very similar to those of Arabs, after all.

They'd have to move soon. There wasn't any anxiety in Harry when he realized that. He looked at his watch and saw the time. Everyone should have been able to get to his place by now. Marty's mortars should be ready. Damn, those were efficient little machines—at least they were in Marty's hands.

They were nothing more than steel tubes. At the bottom were little pins that set off the shells when you dropped them down the opening and . . . *Bam*, off went the rounds. The only problem with them was their uncertain accuracy at any distance like this. Unless Marty was the one handling them, that is.

Harry shook his head. One of the many burdens he'd been given in this life was to be Marty Appelbaum's closest pal. He hadn't really tried to make it happen. It was just that Harry was such a quiet guy that he never said much, even when the runt's constant bantering went on and on and made any other man crazy. *But*—Harry smiled again—*I'm already insane, so it doesn't matter.* Just because he didn't treat Marty with the verbal and often physical abuse Appelbaum had come to expect, he was made Best Friend.

Well, someone had to be. And Harry had such lowered expectations of life that he was perfectly willing to have that burden as well.

Another check of his watch. Just about now . . .

The shells came in with astonishing speed. There were only three mortars, Harry knew that. As well conditioned as the Berets were, that was the most they had been able to carry in along with ammunition on their backpacks. But Marty was at the controls. He had undoubtedly lined them up and carefully stacked the shells, making sure they were not only within easy reach but also that they were aesthetically arranged. It was a prelude to one of his masterpieces, after all. Beauty was important.

Harry watched the line of explosions march in amazing precision from one end of the camp to the other. The point of the attack was to destroy the buildings. The men inside—if they survived—would be forced into the open. There was also the chance that they'd hit the fuel in just the wrong way. But it was unlikely the bombs had been activated here in the desert. It would have made it much too difficult to transport them. They weren't intended for use in warfare on this barren landscape.

Pow! Crump! Harry watched the march of the shells as they moved in a straight line across the Palestinian camp.

Barrrroooommm!

Harry felt a tug in his chest. Marty had just hit something out of the ordinary. It could just have been the Arabs' ammunition cache or it could have been . . . No, it was just conventional arms going up. He could make out the crazy firing of unaimed rounds as they were set off by the heat of the explosions.

The camp was a mass of confusion. Men were crawling out of the huts. They were bleeding, some of them were holding on to the parts of their bodies that had been ripped apart by the explosions. Most were looking to the sky, training their useless rifles on the phantom aircraft that they were sure must be causing this attack. Nothing but a bomber could have performed the surgical precision of the explosions.

They hadn't come up against Marty Appelbaum before, that was all.

The continuing *Pops* of the rounds set off in the ammunition dump only confused the Arabs more. If they were smart enough to realize there wasn't an air attack, they were convinced by the sounds they heard that there was a massive ground assault going on. They were taking cover wherever they could. Their panic had made them stupid.

Harry watched as one group of them hid behind a line of semi-armored vehicles. That was too bad, he thought to himself. He could see movement off to the side now, away from the center of the camp. The camouflage uniforms were working well. If Harry hadn't been looking specifically for his target, he wouldn't ever have seen it. But it was Rosie, his black face barely visible against the white of the Sahara Desert.

He was moving toward the Arabs, who had their backs to him. *Rosie, it's too easy*, Harry said to himself. The terrorists were still studying the source of the small bursts of ammunition. They hadn't realized that it was all unimportant. They were pressed to the sides of the vehicles, waiting for some enemy to make himself known to them.

The enemy was behind them, training his Vz25 at the gasoline tanks that they were stupidly using for protection. It took only a short burst of the automatic weapon to pierce the metal skin of the tanks.

The gasoline went up with a *Whooosh*. It was a soft, almost elegant sound, a nice accompaniment to Appelbaum's ongoing symphony of destruction. It was like a light show added to the percussion instruments. The sounds meant death to the Arabs.

But it wasn't going to be a nice death, neither quick nor calm. It was the worst death that Harry could think of. Burning alive, being just conscious enough to realize that the flaming liquids weren't going to go away and that you couldn't escape them.

He watched as one young man tried hopelessly to rip the clothing from his body. Harry registered a slight amount of sadness when he realized it was only a kid—probably no more than twenty years old. He had torn the shirt off his back and was still screaming as his skin began to blister from the flames. The gasoline had soaked through the fabric and had covered his flesh. There'd be no relief—none.

It had been the true horror of napalm in Vietnam. That had been one of the things that had gotten to the American public, who had seen the war as some kind of continuing docudrama on their television sets. The evening news had become just another serial for their night's entertainment. But every population has some standards of decency, and napalm had been the American public's limit.

Death by fire was something too horrible for most of them to be willing to witness. They saw little children running naked down village streets with globs of the petroleum-based stuff clinging to their skin and they said *Enough*. Fire meant hell. Fire meant intolerable pain. Fire meant screams and yells of agony.

Just like those that were coming out of the mouth of the Arab youth. Harry wished that he was closer. If he could have, he would have shot the boy and put him out of his misery. But he was too far away and Rosie was too intent on the rest of his job—shooting the life out of the rest of them.

If there had been even more gasoline on the young man's body, things would have been easier. If there had been enough to suck the oxygen out of his lungs, then he could have suffocated and the excruciating pain of the flames wouldn't have gotten to him.

Harry watched as the young Arab fell to the ground. He was moving, but it seemed to be just the automatic spasms of his muscles as the brain ceased to send them messages. He was dead. Gone. Somewhere there was a mother who was going to be mourning her baby. Somewhere there was a father who would never see his grandchildren born and a girl who wouldn't get to have that dreamed-of wedding day.

Harry stood up and began to run down the ridge into the village. It was his turn now. The Vz25 was loaded and ready and he was joining the party. He was coming from the Arabs' blind side. They had all been either still facing the ammunition dump and its incoherent shots or else had turned to face the assault from Rosie. None of them were ready for Harry or for Beeker, who was coming toward the same point from a slightly different perspective.

They weren't listening carefully. If they had, they might have been able to discern a difference between the erratic firings from the ammunition cache and the carefully aimed and perfectly placed rounds that Beeker and Harry were sending into their midst.

One after another, the Arabs fell. Their heads were bursting like melons and their chests were opening like slit sides of beef as the bullets tore through them. They were all specially manufactured hot rounds, prefragmented hollow tips that made them go off like small bombs when they hit a target.

Harry sent off a short burst from his automatic weapon and saw the bullets rip apart a man who had turned and was about to get off one round at the attacking Black Berets. He was dead before his finger could pull the trigger. Harry was just a little bit glad that the man had died so quickly and easily. At least, Harry thought, the man didn't have to suffer the fate of burning to death.

That thought made it even easier for Harry to turn to his right and stop three Arabs cold as they tried to run from the camp.

4

Rosie looked at the scene of destruction all around him. They weren't going to be able to stay here long. They had to assume that there had been a chance for someone in the Palestinian camp to get off a rapid message to alert Qadhafi's troops. He couldn't help but scan the sky to see if a MIG wasn't going to come flying down on them.

The sounds of the interrogation brought his attention back down to earth. Al-Kaldi, the most feared Arab terrorist in the world, was sitting cross-legged in the middle of what had been his camp. He was scowling, not at all pleased by the turn of events that left him a captive in the hands of unknown enemies.

Too, bad, sweetheart, Rosie said to himself as he looked at the Arab chief's discomfort. *Surprised you didn't wet your pants.* Lots of people did that when they were really scared. Rosie just took it for granted that some captives were going to pee on themselves. It wasn't a pretty sight to see, and it sure could smell bad, but that was the way it happened in the real world.

Rosie knew all about the real world. He knew about the streets of Harlem and the worse ones that crisscrossed downtown

Newark, where he'd grown up. He knew about the filthy alley-ways where two-bit whores sold their flesh, the only commodity they ever had that was worth even a couple of bucks to anyone else. He knew it all.

He also knew about war. The camp where he now stood was a scene that he'd witnessed repeatedly all over the globe. In a matter of less than an hour there'd be a smell to the place. The flesh would begin to rot under the bright sun; the blood was already congealing on the bodies of the dead and wounded. The carrion eaters were starting to gather.

Even here in the Sahara there were always vultures ready to come down and clean the flesh off the bones of the dead. Amazing, Rosie thought. It was just downright amazing that the birds existed even here.

But then they were in good company. Rosie looked back at al-Kaldi and wished that Beeker would hurry up with his questions. There wasn't just the opportunity that Rosie might have to work on the terrorist himself—he was the acknowledged torture expert among the Black Berets—but there was also the chance they could just blow this desert spot and get their asses home to Louisiana where they belonged.

But Beeker seemed to be doing his thing just as he wanted to. Rosie knew better than to interfere with the leader of the Black Berets while he was trying to get information out of an enemy. It was just that al-Kaldi *deserved* to be turned over to Rosie.

The big black man reached into the sheath on the side of his belt and felt the fine Czech steel blade that was there waiting to be used on some piece of scum like this Arab idiot who was making his mark on world history by murdering little babies and their mamas.

The images of the busload of Israeli children in France

came back to Rosie. Men in battle were there because they were soldiers. They took their chances. Sometimes you win and sometimes—even if you're a Black Beret—you lose. That was the way of the world and Rosie accepted it. But he did not accept the idea that children sometimes had to be among the losers.

Rosie was thinking back to those cadavers in Newark that he used to peel apart for the surgeons who used the skin to save children's lives. He wanted to do that with al-Kaldi. It wasn't that he would get great pleasure from it. He wouldn't mind, of course, but inflicting pain wasn't something that Rosie actually enjoyed. He wasn't a sadist, he was a soldier. It just seemed to him that justice would be best served, though, if this piece of dead meat that called himself a freedom fighter got to sense what pain was really all about. Rosie didn't want to inflict the pain for his own enjoyment, he just thought it could represent a good lesson in manners for al-Kaldi.

Beeker moved away from the Arab now. Rosie felt his blood start to move more quickly. This might be his chance! The half-breed moved over to the big man and shook his head. "There's nothing here. Not a damn thing."

"Are you sure, Billy Leaps? Are you sure that this guy isn't just covering something up from you? If I could just take a few minutes with him . . ."

"No," Beeker said. "He isn't smart enough to comprehend the questions I'm asking. He doesn't know shit about atomic bombs."

"What about the rest of them here? The other ones?"

"They were supposed to be Basque." Beeker was puzzled by something. "But they say they're from the Lusitanian Liberation Front. What the hell is that?"

"Give me a few minutes with al-Kaldi and I'll find out."

Beeker didn't even hear Rosie's suggestion. "They're all

members of the group that got the bus. We don't have explicit orders, but I don't see any option right now. We have to get the fuck out of this mess and fast. We don't have time for little friends to follow us or talk to the Libyans."

"Want to give Appelbaum a shot at them?" Rosie asked. He knew damn well that the terrorists in this camp were criminals. Any civilized nation on earth would have delivered a death penalty to them without a dissenting vote from the jury. But after the bus attack it seemed only right that Appelbaum, the one Jew among them, would be the one who got to pull the trigger.

"No," Beeker said. "We're soldiers, not executioners."

"Beeker, after what they did . . ."

"I have a better idea."

There were seven men still living. Harry had insisted on being able to go among the bodies strewn around the ground with his Czech pistol. As the rest of the Black Berets went to work on the living Arabs, their labors were punctuated with the sounds of Harry's pistol going off at irregular intervals.

When he was done and came to join the rest of them, there were tears running down Harry's cheeks. His eyes were so swollen and his mustache so wet, Rosie knew that Harry had been crying the whole time he'd been at his mission. The rest of them would have let the mortally wounded men die excruciating deaths. But Harry had insisted on delivering the coup de grace to each of them. He had demanded that the men, so many of them so young, each receive the luxury of a single shot in the temple to put him out of the lagging misery.

Rosie didn't always understand Harry. Harry could be a hard man when he had to—he wouldn't hesitate. But give him a chance to be soft and he'd take it. No matter what the cost to himself.

There was no doubt that what he'd just done would cost

Harry. None at all. The images of the dying men he had just dispatched into a welcome, painless death would haunt the man for the rest of his life. The pictures would join the horror show that made up Harry's nightmares. God only knew what other dark visions were in there. Rosie only shrugged. If Harry wanted it, Harry could have it.

He turned his attention to the other task at hand. He quickly stripped out of the desert camouflage uniform they'd worn and tossed it aside. It felt pretty good to be naked in the desert, feeling all that sun beat down on his skin, just like it had on his ancestors. The dry heat evaporated the sweat that had been rolling off his skin. He could feel it rise up and disappear into the air.

He reached down and picked up one of the military outfits that al-Kaldi's men had been wearing. They'd been lucky to find a few men nearly as big as Harry and Rosie. That was unusual. There weren't that many men as big as Rosie and Harry. Or Beeker for that matter.

Rosie pulled on the pants and buttoned the fly. He took a T-shirt and, ignoring the single clean bullet hole that had gone through the chest just where the man's heart would have been, pulled that over his head. The burnoose was the best part of the Palestinian rig. The long piece of cloth wrapped around Rosie's head and gave him vital protection from the sun's rays.

He found a military jacket and put that on, completing the outfit. His own boots were good enough for now. When Rosie stood up he discovered that all the other Black Berets were dressed. Harry was putting the last touches on Marty's outfit.

"I don't like wearing this shit," Appelbaum was complaining as the burnoose was wrapped around his skull. "It's anti-Semitic."

"Marty," Harry said with the tone of a sigh that was usual with his speech, "you're a Semite."

"That's a gross thing to say." Marty pulled away from his pal and stared his watery blue eyes at him. "I'm a Jew, how can I—"

"Jews are Semites, Marty." Harry ignored the temper tantrum and picked up the flowing length of material and began wrapping it again. "All your ancestors wore this kind of thing while they were tending their flocks—just like mine in Greece."

"Well," Marty said with an edge of distrust, "if you say so."

"I do."

When they were finished they walked over to Beeker, who was facing the now-naked Arab captives. Al-Kaldi looked a lot less fearsome with his pecker hanging out than he had with all the stuff of war on his person. But there was still that bit of ego, that look of command, that most military commanders have and are able to keep in the worst of circumstances.

"Do what you will," the Arab said in nearly perfect English. "I am prepared to die for the cause."

"Don't worry about it, you're not going to, at least not right away," Beeker announced. He nodded to the others, who sprang into action and went about the plan Beeker had come up with.

The Arabs were used to the heat of the desert. But one of their keys to survival was their knowledge of how to compensate for the climate. They usually wore layers of clothing that covered nearly all of their body surfaces. That kept in the vital liquids. If they had to, they could even reach into their garments and find those places where their sweat had gathered and suck the life-giving fluid until they found a more normal source of water.

The worst thing to do in the desert was to expose your skin. It drew out liquids, for one thing. For another, human skin wasn't built to take the naked rays of the equatorial sun. But now the Black Berets were binding the nude Arabs to the skeletons of their old vehicles. They were going to leave them here, spread over the burning hot steel and defenseless against the Saharan day.

Al-Kaldi knew what it meant. Death would come slowly, it would crawl over him, moving inch by inch, taking his spirit to places of unimaginable terror before he would ever have the release of death. If no one came to find him before he passed into Allah's hands, there would be no worse way for him to leave this earth.

"You killed the others quickly," al-Kaldi pleaded with Harry. "Why won't you do that for me? Why this?"

"Because of the little babies." That was all Harry said.

"You fools!" al-Kaldi was screaming at the whole troop of Black Berets as they gathered up their packs and started to make their way out of the Palestinian camp. "You think you've ended my campaign!"

Rosie turned and looked at another man who was now draped over the hulk of an East German personnel carrier beside him. "You wouldn't even know what a real soldier does, you scum."

Rosie meant it. He'd seen the work of the "terrorists" of the world. He'd even seen it happen in the United States when some stupid-ass blacks thought that the way to "liberate" themselves was to burn down the ghettos where their families lived and where poor blacks were struggling to survive. *Destroy.* That was the motto of these "freedom fighters."

"My people will rise up and they will avenge my death."

"They gonna kill some more children? Maybe they'll take out a group of housewives instead," Rosie taunted the helpless man.

"Idiot," al-Kaldi snarled at him. "The rule of terror will come. Disorder will reign and the righteous will rise up with the help of God, whose messenger was Allah."

"Don't you talk to me about Allah," Rosie said. "I've heard all I need to about the fool who's brought such death and destruction to innocent people. You and your kind don't understand—fighting is something that we have fighting men for. There are battles for soldiers, not for civilians."

"You're the one who doesn't understand," al-Kaldi said. "The armies of the liberation will come into your cities. They will burn your houses and they will bomb your hospitals. If the people of Palestine and the other occupied territories of the world cannot have peace, then no one shall have peace."

"Have nice daydreams, pal," Rosie said. The others had begun to march away. "The sun will help your mind work a lot better than it has been in the past few years. I got work to do right now."

Rosie started to make his way through the desert. The others were aways ahead of him now. The shouts of al-Kaldi came after him. Rosie knew what was getting to the man. He had probably dreamed of his glorious death in battle. He had thought about his martyrdom as a glamorous event that would be told and retold after he'd gone. That dream had been taken away from him.

He was just another scared person who was going to die a hard death—the sun was going to cook his skin. It would blister painfully and he'd have to watch the vultures who'd gathered in the sky knowing that they might not wait. They could dive down and start to peck at his eyes. Those tasty morsels might look so good to them that they would be willing to take the chance that al-Kaldi couldn't defend himself.

Rosie knew about fear. He'd seen it. He'd seen it so close up that he had long ago lost the image of a glorious death. There was no such thing. There was only the reality that it was all going to be over someday.

He got up to the others and slowed down to match their pace. He looked at Harry and Cowboy, Beeker and Marty and he knew that they had all looked the Big D in the eyes as well.

It was something they lived with. There was no glory that could ever compensate for it—not ever. There was only the final reality.

Rosie didn't want to think more about that. He was wondering what Beeker's next move was going to be. These terrorists hadn't been the ones. They had known there was the possibility that this wasn't their target. But they had to keep on looking.

Someone out there who wasn't on their side had a set of atomic bombs. Those bombs could be used to end the earth. That would be the one real Big D—death for the whole human race. They had to find them and they had to stop them from ever being used.

Al-Kaldi's screams became softer and softer as the Black Berets moved into the desert.

Too bad, Rosie thought. *Man shouldn't waste his energy yelling like that. He should conserve his strength.*

5

Marty was furious. *Pissed!* What right did they have to complain? What was the problem? That he'd done his job too well? If they had wanted a frigging vehicle left over from the mortar attack he'd launched, they should have been more careful to tell him so. Was it a crime that he'd done his job too well?

Evidently. They certainly were angry enough with him now. He clenched his small, receding jaw and refused to acknowledge the grief they were giving him. They had no right to assume that at least one vehicle would have survived Marty's assault, no right at all. Once the Rembrandt of destruction was set to work, he *worked*.

They were like his mother. He glowered at the memory of the woman back in New Jersey who took his money when he was foolish enough to make one of his journeys to the hometown and try to show her what a success he was. The last time he'd bought her a new VCR and a large-screen television to go with it. She'd sorted through the Doris Day movie cassettes he'd gotten for her and slipped one into the slot in the recorder.

"Nice machine, very nice machine." She had said it

grudgingly, almost as though it hurt her, like some kind of toothache or something. Then she'd sat down and, while watching that blue-eyed WASP singing some melody about the joys of suburban life, she'd regaled Marty with stories about how well his brothers, the *professionals*, were doing.

"Bet they don't buy you things like this," he'd bragged.

"But their money is honest," his mother had replied with a wide-open expression. "Honest people couldn't afford to squander their money on foolishness like this."

"Do you want me to take it back?" Marty had screamed at her.

She'd looked at him with that long-suffering face of hers. "You always do that, offer me something and then want to take it away from me. After the trouble you caused as a child, always sickly, and the labor pains!"

He was well past thirty and his mother was still complaining about how difficult labor had been! Damn, these Black Berets were no different, though. You try to do something right— the way he'd used those mortars as though they were the most highly advanced weapons on earth—and it's *your fault* if you get all the cars, trucks, and half-tracks in the camp. Just like his mother, who would complain because Marty would buy her gifts more extravagant than any others she ever received and then—when he couldn't really explain how he got the money for them—she'd assume that they were bought with money he didn't earn honestly.

Sure, Mom, he thought to himself, *it's simple. I fight people for money and I blow up enemy installations in the middle of African deserts and I get paid millions in the spoils of war. We collect the treasuries of drug traffickers, we confiscate the bankrolls of terrorists, we make our dollars the old-fashion way—we take them.*

"Goddamnit!" Marty exploded all of a sudden. The others

turned and looked at him, wondering what was getting to the runt this time. "It's not my fault!"

"Come on, Marty," Harry said, taking ahold of Appelbaum's shoulder. "Let's keep marching. We'll find something soon enough."

And every minute that we have to march through the desert they're going to complain that it's my responsibility just because they didn't have a Cadillac limousine waiting at the end of it all . . .

In another hour they found what they were looking for. They nearly stumbled onto it. They had been following a path parallel to a halfway decent road from the Palestinian encampment. Whatever else he did with the money that oil brought to Libya, Qadhafi had built highways.

This was proof that Colonel Qadhafi spent his money on more than public works. He also made sure his treasury provided him with the finest ComBloc weapons possible.

There was a single T-80 battle tank sitting on the side of the road. Around it a bunch of Libyan soldiers—obviously the tank's crew—were taking a lunch break. The tank was just what the Black Berets needed. Beeker looked at the rest of them and they all nodded in silent and unanimous agreement.

They would take it. The crew couldn't have been alerted about the attack on al-Kaldi's camp. They would have been more vigilant if they had.

While the rest of the Black Berets took up positions behind the rise that overlooked the tank's resting place, Rosie was their decoy. It was his usual duty. He never minded this. Being on the front line was always better than waiting under cover. He would always take action over anything else, they all would. Besides, this was a role he was optimally suited for.

Rosie had a big grin on his face as he sauntered down the

slope of the hill toward the T-80 and its resting crew. He was whistling a tune and appeared not to have a care in the world.

"*Mes amis!*" he cried out in the closest approximation of French he could muster.

The Libyans looked up and stared for a moment, then waved him on. While Qadhafi was mainly interested in having his country used as a jumping-off spot for other nationals to make their terrorist attacks on the world, his personal little army would occasionally be sent on its own adventures. The longest lasting and the deadliest had been a covert invasion of Chad, a former French colony that bordered on Libya.

Rosie was the one of the Berets who was always presenting himself as a fellow soldier of liberation to the terrorists they had to deal with. It seemed that the fools couldn't ever quite believe that there were black Americans—and whatever else they saw when they looked at Rosie, they knew he was black—and their guard was always down. Rosie thought that was too bad. There were plenty of Vietcong who could have told these stupid Arabs that there were plenty of black men who were willing, ready, and able to fight under the American flag.

So today he was a Chad freedom fighter. His grin grew more broad and his wave became more exaggerated. Where the hell was Chad exactly? He never did get his modern geography right, what with the way they were always coming up with new names for perfectly well-known places and all. Well, it wasn't going to matter very much in a minute—certainly not to the Libyans.

When he got close enough to take a good look at the T-80, Rosie let out a more sincere whistle. This was one of the most up-to-date versions. The Russkies had loaded this one with Kobra antitank missiles, the kind that had a range of over 3,000 meters. If he remembered right, it wasn't powered by the un-trustworthy V-12 diesel, either. It had a new gas turbine engine that meant it could get some speed here in the desert. What a nice little ride they were going to have today.

Rosie broke out in laughter, he was so happy! He was damned tired of having to march on the desert floor.

He kept yapping some gibberish that was supposed to approach French, but he didn't know what the hell he was saying. The Libyans seemed to be buying his act, though. They were laughing and pointing at him and talking away in Arabic. There were five men in the crew. Good, that's how many the new crew was going to be. He just hoped that Cowboy could figure out how to fire up the new engine.

The oldest of the Libyans seemed to be the one in the least good humor. He barked something at the rest and they suddenly went all serious on Rosie. He wondered what it was. He had a Czech rifle and a Czech pistol in his holster. He was wearing clothes that had no markings on them, but they certainly should have been authentic since he'd gotten them off of a Palestinian.

He actually took a quick look down at himself to see what the matter could possibly be. It all looked cool to him. He had great faith in his acting abilities. He'd been mimicking that he was lost, separated from a detachment that had been on training maneuvers. It had been his attempt to communicate with body language and his nonexistent French that had caused the other Libyans so much merriment.

Then the message got received.

The Libyan officer ran out a line of French so fast and apparently so flawless that Rosie was amazed. The guy sounded as though he'd just walked out of the Sorbonne, he was so fluent. Now who the hell expected a goddamn Libyan to speak French? The old colonial power had been Italy; the current military ally was Russia; the biggest trading partner was West Germany, and this *fool* was talking French!

Rosie was furious. He was so livid that he just took his Vz25 and held it at his hip, a move so nonchalant that no one else noticed it. It seemed utterly unthreatening. And it was. Because Rosie didn't have time to try to intimidate anyone. He only had time to do his job.

And his job meant that a quick and deadly burst of automatic 9-mm rounds went flying through the air and exploded in the Libyan officer's chest.

The rest of the poor fools were frozen for one second. They saw the hot rounds of bullets rip through their comrade's body and leave ugly open craters all over the top half of his torso. Only soldiers like the Black Berets were so inured to the horrors of war that they could look on a sight like that and not respond with total disbelief and at least a little bit of shock.

It was too bad. It was a shame. Because those seconds that they hesitated made up all the time that Rosie needed to turn around and make a sweep of the four men that were still standing. The Vz25 can get off thousands of rounds in the blink of an eye. Many, many more than are necessary to kill four unprepared Libyans.

When it was done and he'd taken his finger off the trigger, Rosie stood back and leaned against the T-80. The Black Berets were running down the slope to join him. He was shaking his head in disbelief that he'd been caught in his act. He hadn't expected to be the one to take out the entire group, but now their bodies were thrown around the clearing, their limbs in impossible positions, their eyes blankly studying the Saharan sun with wide-open lids that would have spelled instant blindness—if they were alive and seeing. But they weren't.

"Go with Allah, babies," Rosie said, giving them a little salute. He only wished he believed there was a god for them to go to.

Cowboy's ability with machines was magical. It helped if they were the kinds that flew in the air. But even if they were earthbound, he could do wonders with anything with an engine in it. It took only about five minutes of checking out the systems of the T-80 to make sure he understood the essential facts about it. He could drive the bastard. He also could read the gauges well enough to understand that there was a good amount of fuel there.

The Kobra missiles were so similar to the type used on the various models of the vaunted Soviet Hind-type helicopter that Cowboy had flown on various missions that he was even going to be able to launch them. They not only had mobility, they had firepower.

Rosie and Beeker had used the short time to study their maps of the region. They saw a direct route between their current position and the Mediterranean coastline about fifty miles away. In between were a number of indications of commercial oil fields.

They were going to have to find the quickest path back to Europe. There hadn't been any hope for an airborne evacuation. The guys who'd taken them in weren't in the least interested in any adventure that involved their landing on Libyan soil. The LA-LO drop was one thing that they'd attempt in their unmarked aircraft. But the exit?

They'd told the Berets that they would have to make their way to the coastline and, by prearranged radio, signal, there would be an amphibious rescue.

Rosie knew that Beeker had hated that term *Rescue*. It just didn't sound military. Hell, the Pentagon would have come up with some godforsaken series of initials to explain it. But the Black Berets weren't into the alphabet game.

It had also been agreed that the Black Berets might try their own evacuation if circumstances allowed it. As the rest of the crew got down in the bowels of the T-80 and Cowboy turned the huge battle tank toward the north, Rosie sat up on top of the turret. Once again his black skin had gotten him a choice opportunity to playact a role as a freedom fighter for the Third World. *Black skin had its advantages once more*, he thought. *Those suckers in the heart of the metal beast are going to swelter and steam and sweat all the way.*

Not Rosie. He had the best seat in the house and he knew it. The breeze caused by the speed of the T-80 ruffled his shirt and kept him cool and happy. There was a big grin on his face as he scoured the horizon. He was on the lookout. It was too early to expect any ocean view. But that didn't mean he wasn't likely to find a nice little way for them to avoid that amphibious rescue shit.

That just didn't sound like the Black Berets' way.

6

There weren't supposed to be any Americans left in Libya. The Arab country's relentless support for terrorists around the world had turned it into an outlaw state as far as Washington was concerned. There had to be an end to any contamination of America through any dealings with the criminal country.

Easy enough said. There was just one problem: oil.

No matter how the prices rose and fell, oil was still the black gold of the twentieth century. Libya was one of its richest fields. As soon as Washington's decree had gone out and thousands of American employees of various countries had left with their dependents, just as many West German, Dutch, and Italian employees took their places, happy not to have to compete with the Americans for the high-paying jobs in the Libyan oil fields.

The T-80 made its way down the highway to the point that both Rosie and Beeker had found on the map. There was supposed to be an Afro-American Oil Company field at the site. They knew that couldn't be. That corporation had been one of the first to follow the federal mandate that it abandon Libya.

But if the wells had been rich enough to attract Afro-American, they were rich enough to have been taken over by someone else.

As soon as they drew close to the camp, Rosie figured that the "someone" else were Italians. It only made sense. Before their defeat in the Second World War, they had ruled Libya as a colony. They hadn't been bad masters, more incompetent than anything else. The Libyans bore them no real animosity. The Italians were welcome, especially once the Americans had left with their technical expertise and their capital investments.

Rome had been happy to increase its already huge investments in Libya. The speed with which the Afro-American Oil Company's logos had been painted over by the Italo-Arab Corporation's was just one small sign.

But Rosie still kept on smiling. He was in glee. He was just as happy as he could be. Because the Italians had brought more than a few new drills and a change in personnel to the field. They'd brought a nice, new, shiny jet airplane.

As the T-80 approached the Italian camp it caused no real notice. They were close enough to Libyan training camps that a tank wouldn't be a cause for alarm or surprise. The workers would be used to it.

Cowboy drove the tank right up to the entrance to the largest of the prefabricated structures that made up the buildings in the field's headquarters. There was a wire fence around the perimeter, but its gate was open. It was probably closed only at night to keep out wandering wild animals and flocks of the local herders' goats who might have gotten too curious about the lights and sounds of the Italians.

Rosie looked around at all the unarmed employees of the firm. It was after quitting time and most were sitting around waiting for the sun to go down, drinking good Italian wine—which was illegal in Islamic Libya but whose existence was overlooked by the gracious hosts—and looking forward to dinner, which was probably going to be presented in whichever of the other buildings was the mess hall.

Rosie climbed down from the tank turret. An official-looking man walked over to him and extended a hand, offering an incomprehensible greeting in Italian. Rosie shook hands with the man and started dreaming about pasta.

But in a flash Beeker was standing beside him. The leader's shirt was soaked with perspiration and he was in a foul mood. Obviously Billy Leaps, who had to have seen the plane on the corporate runway, had decided that this wasn't the time to play with the Italians.

While Rosie listened to Beeker's angry and tired tone of voice as he and the Italian official tried to find a common language, he realized that the leader was anxious to get the hell out of here. Not a bad idea as far as Rosie was concerned. Not a bad idea at all.

He walked back over to the tank while the two men, obviously giving up on the idea of being able to communicate with one another, went to find an interpreter. Rosie didn't know any language that would help them out. He would just lean against the T-80 and look at the people milling about.

The rest of the Berets had climbed out of the heated entrails of the huge machine and were moving around, happy to get any relief from the stifling heat that they'd been trapped in. Damn Russkies might have built a fine fighting machine, but they sure hadn't thought about passenger comfort when they were doing it.

Cowboy was the only one who jumped down onto the ground and seemed to be in peak shape while he took in the sight of the couple of dozen Italians who were loitering around the oil camp. "Are there any women, Rosie? Huh? Are there any women at all?"

Rosie sighed and shook his head. Cowboy would never learn. His one great weakness was Latin ladies—all kinds of Latin ladies, though he did have a marked preference for the ones that lived in South America. In fact, his preference had been so well focused that he had married more than a few of them.

Cowboy had never bothered with the niceties of divorce or any of that. No, no, not their Cowboy. He believed so fervently in love that it wounded his romantic soul to think that legal issues could ever enter into the conversation.

Love! It was what the fly-boy lived for, even more than his coke, even more than the controls of the state-of-the-art aircraft he was always admiring, he was in love with love.

It had caused the Black Berets more than a few troubles. That tendency of his not to worry about divorces was something that they understood about their friend, but the fathers of many of the women involved—as well as the brothers, uncles, and most male cousins—didn't quite see it the same way. All they saw was betrayal.

It wasn't that. Rosie knew that Cowboy's heart was in the right place. It was something else. Cowboy was so in love with the perfection of romance that whenever the ugly realities of existence intruded on it, well, he had to leave.

But before he did he would pay careful and close and heartfelt attention to the process of courtship. He loved courtship and all the little cooings and eyelid flutterings that came with it.

And he was a genius when it came to planning marriages. After all, a marriage is the proof of two people's adoration of one another. Even more, he lived for honeymoons. The image of two lovebirds sitting in a hotel suite far from the crowds and ugliness of day-to-day life, sipping champagne with their room-service breakfast in preparation for one more physical manifestation of their vows—*that* was something worth living for.

In fact, it was something so worth living for that Cowboy had arranged for at least two dozen honeymoons for himself and his many beloveds.

But then, sad to say, Rosie knew that there would come the remark that would start the end. It would be so innocent. The girl might say something about Cowboy attending a family event. She might hint that her daddy was willing to give him a job. Or she might wonder where the money was going to come from to pay for this wonderful hotel room.

What none of them understood was one simple fact: Love was a fantasy. At least to Cowboy. Love shouldn't have any reality to it. It should be weddings with nice flowers and deep-voiced priests. It should be receptions with smiling families. It should be honeymoons with endless sex and romance.

It shouldn't deal with future plans. It shouldn't be concerned with family relations. It shouldn't need crass folding money to make it work. It should just . . . *be.*

The minute the Latin ladies forgot that was the minute Cowboy went over the top. He would disappear into the night and never return. He could only hope that the women would eventually decide that they had had as much fun with him as he had had with them.

Maybe, Rosie thought, *just maybe it was true.* But the simple reality was that nothing would ever stop Cowboy from his quest for another night with another Latin lady. As soon as he had seen the Italian flag that flew over the camp he must have started wishing and hoping that there would be a potential conquest for him.

Cowboy was beginning to get upset as he prowled around the tank and searched the camp area. There was nothing, nothing at all! There were just men here. "What, are all Italians faggots?" he demanded with a hurt voice.

"Don't know about that," Rosie said. "I never did have reason to look into it."

"How can they stand being here without any women?" he demanded.

"Did you ever stop to think," Rosie said softly, "just what that private airplane is doing here? Could it just be that these men are smart enough to bring their women into a country that makes a national pastime out of war? Couldn't it especially make sense that they'd do that since their homeland isn't more than ninety miles across the Mediterranean from here? How much time does it take to fly that in a job like this one?" Rosie pointed to the Aerospatiale craft on the runway.

"You're right." The gleam in Cowboy's eye came back. "You're absolutely right. Sicily is directly across from this point of Libya. Why, we could be there in half an hour in this thing."

"I think you just understood why there aren't any Italian ladies here in camp, Cowboy."

"But there *are* millions of them—*millions*—less than an hour away!"

Rosie was honestly happy for his pal. It would be a lot easier on all of them if Cowboy could find someone to play kissing games with in a place like Sicily where they were very unlikely ever to show their faces again. It was getting to be a bitch remembering just which Latin American cities they had to watch out for angry daddies in.

Beeker came storming across the field from the headquarters building. His uniform had already begun to dry in the arid Saharan air. "Cowboy, let's go. Here's the flight plan."

"Where to?" the pilot asked.

"Palermo. We're expected."

"These guys are just going to let us fly out of here in their toy?"

"They talked to a few very nice people back in Rome who

thought it might not be a bad idea to earn a few rental dollars after they'd investigated a little of our background with some other friends in Washington. You can fly this thing, can't you?"

Cowboy was as hurt as Marty would have been if Beeker had asked him if he could pull the pin on a hand grenade. "Of course I can!"

"Then let's get the fuck out of here," Billy Leaps said. "Even the Libyans are going to eventually put together a couple of things and realize that the raid on the Palestinian camp has something to do with the disappearance of this damn tank. Come on, boy, let's get flying."

"To Palermo!" The sound of the Italian city just rolled off Cowboy's lips.

"For a couple of minutes," Beeker announced. "Seems we have a different final destination."

"Beeker!" The sound coming out of Cowboy's throat now was one of utter torture. "You're going to take me into Sicily, the land of my dreams, the place where I'm sure to finally find *her*, and then you're going to expect me to just leave?"

"Get your ass moving, Cowboy. I think you'll be perfectly happy with where we're going to end up. Happier than I'll be, that's for damn sure. The frigging place isn't any closer to Louisiana than we are now. Goddamn it. Come on, let's get moving."

7

"So this is Lusitania." Billy Leaps Beeker was staring out over the balcony.

Delilah came up close to him. He wished she wouldn't do that. Her smell was hitting him like a fist in the stomach. How long had it been since he had a woman? He didn't even try to figure it out. It was too long. Here, beside him, was the one he wanted more than any other. He hated that—maybe he even hated her because of it.

"That's what the Romans called Portugal," Delilah explained. "It was probably the name of one of the tribes they found here when they conquered it."

The ancient city of Oporto was sprawled out beneath them. Its once-great harbor was blocked by a sandbar, a living piece of geography much like the shifting desert they'd left in Africa not long ago. But the water of the Atlantic was blue and inviting. It would be cool, maybe even cold, and Beeker liked that idea after the effect that Delilah was having on him.

"What makes you think this is the place?" He tried to get back to business, hoping that it would take his mind off the proximity of the body he knew only too well. "This is a long way from the Libyan Desert. You were sure the target was there."

His turn to serious subjects worked—at least for a little while. Delilah might be the single most sensuous woman he'd ever met, but when Beeker mentioned an assignment, she was all business. Her posture changed; she stood up, away from the railing of the balcony. She didn't look at him now, but she did explain:

"We had reports that al-Kaldi was preparing the most dramatic terrorist strike of his life. He'd been bragging about it to everyone he could. The operation was supposed to be the largest move toward Palestinian independence yet. We thought—and we had so much corroborating evidence it seemed to be sure—that he was going to use the atomic weapons against Israel.

"He's that type, the kind that thinks you can destroy something in order to take it away from someone else and forget that—since you destroy it—you can't have it yourself when it's all said and done. His hatred of Israel and everyone who's ever supported it in any way was so intense that we had to take into account the probability that he'd try everything in his power to set the bombs off there."

"I can believe it," Beeker said, remembering the crazed speeches the doomed Arab leader had made as the Black Berets left him to his slow death in the oven of the desert.

"Everything pointed to him. But it wasn't him, you've proven that."

"Is this just another wild-goose chase? Just because there were some jokers in training who called themselves the 'Lusitanian Liberation Front' is no reason to get us here, to Portugal."

"No, there's more, much more."

"I'm listening, lady."

She shifted now and turned to look him in the eye. "This country is naked. In the past ten days every single British,

American, and French intelligence agent in Portugal has been compromised. *Every single one!*"

"The Soviets got you, huh?" He almost seemed happy about the CIA being caught with its pants down.

"Hardly, Beeker. They're naked too. As far as we can tell, every East Bloc agent in Portugal has been decommissioned."

"What the hell does that mean?"

"It means that someone has gone about the business of blowing the cover of every major secret agent in Portugal. It's been a brilliant maneuver. Those of us who can only guess what's happened because we're so far away from the scene of the action have been looking on with awe.

"There's not a hint of it in the press. It's been done too subtly. But it's been done with deadly seriousness. Some agents were simply killed. But it was made to look as though the murders were acts of random violence or else, because the spies involved were using the underworld as their own shield against notice, the shootings have looked like gangland murders.

"Others have been compromised in other ways. There was one man—a Russian, surprisingly not a Brit—who was supposed to be the ladies' man of Lisbon. Somehow they managed to get him into a brothel full of boys and they also were able to coordinate a police raid on the place when he—coincidentally—was in it. There were press photographers. It might be that Moscow did him in themselves, but it appears that the suicide that resulted was more likely to be authentic.

"There were less violent acts as well. Businessmen were recalled home by corporate headquarters. Fishermen who were recording the comings and goings of NATO ships for the Russians lost their boats. An airline pilot was a courier for the French part-time; his plane blew up on takeoff from Orly. A jeweler was the banker for the CIA in the Algarve region; he was raided by the local police and counterfeit money was discovered. It was definitely a plant, but now he's in jail.

"The list goes on and on, Beeker. The country was swept clean. This is the only place in all of Europe where the watching eyes aren't functioning. The shock waves are still surging through the world's capitals. This isn't supposed to be happening."

"Well, it looks like your Portuguese allies must have helped it all along."

"Not a single bit. Not at all. At least we can't discover it. Portugal has just become a democracy in the past few years. For decades before that it was under the rule of Salazar, one of the most vicious dictators in the world when he was alive and in charge. In those days nothing could have happened without his permission and his complicity. His successor, Caetano, was only a little bit better. But the new regime is bending over backward not to break the rules. The arrests and the raids all came in response to anonymous tips. There's no indication of any conspiracy at the national level.

"Someone very smart and very well connected knew exactly what was going on with the intelligence apparatus of every one of the great powers. When that person needed to he wiped out the whole thing in less than a week."

"You jokers can replace all of them in a day. What's your problem?"

"No. They can't be replaced in a day. I'm sure the others are working as hard as we are to do what they can right now, and I'm sure we'll all be functioning at least partially in a couple of weeks. That's not the point. The point is more crucial. For the past two weeks no one knows what's been going on in Portugal.

"I told you, the place has been naked. The Lusitanian Liberation Front was just a little bit more, a small piece of confirmation."

"So you think your bombs are here." He was scowling at the thought. *The bombs that will take away my son's future.* "How did you ever let those things get stolen, anyhow? I thought atomic bombs would be under such strong security—if there's such a thing left in the world—that they couldn't just be walked off with."

The topic obviously got to her. She sucked in her breath between clenched teeth. "They didn't get bombs. What they got was Uranium-235. That came from the States. They stole polonium from West Germany. And lithium from Great Britain. All the materials were supposed to be under the tightest possible controls.

"But they weren't actual bombs yet. They were still just raw materials. There were mistakes made."

"Mistakes like that are pretty dangerous, lady. How come the press isn't crawling all over you?"

"Only the U-235 would have really alerted the press. We never released the story—a matter of national security. The rest of the thefts were minor issues of industrial espionage. No one reacted to them. Thank God. If the public knew that there were atomic bombs out there—"

"Wait a minute," Beeker broke in. "If there aren't really bombs, what's going on? I thought you had to have a thousand PhDs to make an atomic bomb."

She wasn't getting any happier with the conversation now. "That was the old days. It's still true for a large and sophisticated weapon. But the truth is that a simple atomic device is so simple to manufacture that almost any undergraduate physics major could do it—given the right materials."

"And they got those."

"That's right, Beeker. They have those. All it takes in addition to the refined uranium, the polonium, and lithium are some pieces of lead to create a casing, about a half pound of plastic explosives, and a detonating device that's available from any mining-supply company in the world."

"And your agents weren't here to watch the pieces get shipped into Portugal. But you said the Portuguese aren't involved, that they're not pulling this off. Then how did everything get by their customs people? Explain that one to me."

"We're not sure. But listen, Beeker, this country lives off the sea. Do you know that the simple fishing boats of the Portuguese, the ones that used to sail out of this very harbor before it was blocked by the sandbars, were drying their cod on the shores of New England centuries before the Pilgrims even thought about taking a little cruise across the Atlantic? There are thousands of fishing vessels that come and go from every village and hamlet up and down the hundreds of miles of coastline here. Even if all of our intelligence networks—the Americans and the Russians and everyone's allies—were functioning, they still could have gotten those materials into the country. The cargoes wouldn't have been large."

"So you think there's someone here in Oporto who wants to make some bombs. Do you think they're going to blow up this country?"

"I don't know. I doubt it. The information we had about al-Kaldi still makes sense, you know. Maybe he was helping out some group here in return for the favor of one of their little presents. Who knows where the rest of them are going to go?

"It's one of the nightmares of the world."

"You mean the western world," Beeker snorted.

"No, Billy Leaps. I mean the world. Why do you think they had to take out the Russians as well? There aren't many things Washington and Moscow are ever going to agree on, but the need to defend civilization against terrorists is one of them. If it ever got to the threat of nuclear terrorism, the KGB would be right beside us, all the way."

"Are you scared?"

"Very. I'm terrified. There's a chance of massive human destruction. Beeker, we're talking about these things as though they were toys because they're so much smaller than the ones that make up the powers' arsenals. But a well-placed bomb set off in London, Paris, or New York could mean millions of lives. And worse, the end of any possibility of world peace."

"You just said the Russkies were on our side. Why do you think—"

"Do you think we could ever convince anyone in real power in Washington that a series of terrorist raids on the major cities of the world weren't Moscow-inspired? And do you think anyone who ever dreamed of being a dove in the Kremlin could ever convince their military brass that we weren't responsible for an atomic bomb going off in the middle of Leningrad?

"Yes, Beeker, I'm scared."

She moved even closer; their elbows touched. A slight shock of electric-like feeling went through Beeker, and if he hadn't had so much pride, he would have pulled away from her. But he didn't want her to know just how much power she had over him. Even though she probably already knew, he wasn't about to give her the evidence that easily.

She leaned her head against his shoulder and the voltage on the electric force he was feeling just got a whole lot higher than it had been before. He tried not to give in to her easily. But there had been such a sincere show of emotion in her talk about the bombs—there had been such naked fear—that he couldn't stop himself from reaching over and running a comforting hand through her hair.

It was all the signal she needed. She shifted her body and those wonderfully firm breasts of hers were pressing against his chest. He wanted to pull away, but he looked down and saw the upturned lips. They had the most delicious flavor in the world. He knew they did. They were soft and they were wet—just like another part of her that he knew very well.

His arms didn't seem to respond to him. They involuntarily wrapped themselves around her trim waist and lifted her up toward him until he could taste her mouth. Then it was all over. He carried her upright, their mouths still clinging to one another, into the hotel room and laid both their bodies on the mattress of the bed.

She was always in control, she was always the proper businesswoman in public. It could infuriate him sometimes. She would transform, though, in moments like this. She would turn herself into some kind of sexually mad female. He watched as she tore at her own clothes, almost ripping them in order to get naked.

She liked that. He'd learned over the years how much she enjoyed stripping in front of him, as though she knew just how much of an advantage it gave her to have him see her nude. There were those breasts with the delicate pink nipples, now hard, signaling just how ready she was for him. And there was the place between her legs.

His mouth felt dry as he looked down there and saw the blond halo of her pubic hair. He could taste those lips too. He knelt at the side of the bed and his hands explored her flesh, running his palms over the cool and firm surface of her belly, her back, and then coming around the front to fondle those wonderful breasts. He knelt up and leaned forward and softly and gently he kissed first one and then the other of the two miracles.

"Hurry," she said. It was a fervent command, an expression of primal need. She pulled back from him and sprawled on her back on the mattress. "Quickly," she whispered in her most urgent, husky voice.

He got up off his knees. It was almost an expression of anger when he pulled open his shirt and then pulled off his undershirt. He kicked away his shoes. He quickly reached down and tore off his socks. Then he undid the button on his fly and let his slacks drop to the floor.

She leaned up now, her hand in front of her in a beseeching posture, as though she were trying to get to the mound trapped in his shorts. It was like she couldn't wait. He wanted to play with her, make her admit out loud how much she wanted it. But he couldn't do it. He just couldn't. He seemed to be disgusted with himself when he took the elastic band of the briefs and pushed them down to the floor. He had no control over his reactions to her. None. His flesh proved it.

He moved to the center of the bed and, on his hands and knees, crawled up into the waiting triangle of her sex. Her hands grabbed hold of his shoulders as soon as she could and she pulled him down, her legs spread wide in her willingness to receive him. He felt the first contact of his need and her wetness. They both moaned, they both were in battle, they both . . .

Then he slipped in and all he could think about was the warmth, the incredible warmth and the sounds of the Atlantic ocean outside their window.

"What was that all about?" he asked.

She rolled over and rested her head on his bare chest. Her eyes had a strange expression to them. It couldn't be hurt, he told himself. Delilah doesn't know what hurt is. It must just be surprise that he called her bluff and let her know that something was wrong with the whole thing.

"What do you mean?"

"The sex. And the things you're not telling me."

"The sex was . . . sex. I wanted it."

That was all she said. There was some little piece of Beeker deep down inside that didn't want to hear her say that. He knew she wouldn't ever be one of the ones who'd lie to him. There'd be no bullshit about it. But he wasn't sure he wanted the truth in that barren a form: *I wanted it.*

"The idea of what might happen just made me feel so vulnerable, so mortal." Her thoughts seemed to drift away. They came back to the present now. "I wanted to touch you the best way I knew how. I wanted to know that your body was still there and I could still feel it."

That was better. He relaxed a little bit. There had been some emotion at least. She wasn't just treating him like some pickup.

He got up and went into the bathroom. He splashed water on his face and studied it in the mirror. It was the same one that looked back at him every morning. No surprises here. None at all. It was just the portrait of a fighter who was putting his life on the line and who had just made love with the one woman in the world he wanted the most. Then why didn't he feel any better?

He took a towel and dried himself off. He went back into the bedroom and discovered her lolling on the bed, a cigarette in her hand. It was one of the many habits of hers that he hated, but he tolerated them in Delilah when he wouldn't have stood for them with anyone else.

He was at the foot of the bed. He wondered—as he did so often—why she didn't feel the need to be more modest, the way other women would act. She had left her legs wide open, not bothering even to pull them together to protect herself from his invading eyes. She was staring out the window, and even though she had to know he was studying her, she didn't make a single effort to hide any part of herself.

8

Rosie thought his heart would fall into pieces. The woman could *wail!*

He sat in the little bar near the ocean in Oporto and listened as the fado singer belted out the torturously sad songs that fed the souls of the Portuguese people. He didn't understand a single goddamn word that she was singing, but he could feel every ounce of the sorrow and the despair.

The woman was attractive, not young, but he liked them that way, a little older, more ripe. They knew things that younger girls don't know. When it comes down to action under the covers when the lights are out, all the pretty looks that the young ones had didn't make a bit of difference. What did count was knowing how to do it. That called for maturity and emotion. This woman had that.

She had glistening dark hair drawn up behind her head. There was some kind of fan contraption holding it together in the back. Her skin wasn't made up, but the dark olive complexion made her more than beautiful enough for Rosie right now.

The guitarist stopped. His head was hanging in grief after

whatever it was the woman had sung to the audience. There was a burst of applause, but it wasn't the enthusiastic clapping that you'd get in the States when someone was done with a set. It was more like a mournful admission that she'd done it, she'd gotten to them. The men, who made up the vast majority of the crowd, were admitting their defeat as much as they were acknowledging her artistry.

Harry was one of them. Rosie looked over at the big Greek and wondered if this was finally going to be the thing that sent him over the edge. They'd listened to the blues together on countless occasions in black clubs in the States and Harry had barely been able to survive. Harry lived the blues, he didn't need to hear them.

Now he had that look on his face that told you he was re-membering every injustice ever committed on every innocent heart in the world. Harry never forgot a one of them. Rosie just shook his head and took another shot of the inexpensive but good Portuguese wine, *vinho verde*, "green wine."

It wasn't really green. They'd explained to him that the name referred to the youth of the grapes and the fact that the wine wasn't allowed to age. Seemed that any people who could listen to this sad shit every night in a bar couldn't afford to give their alcohol time to mellow. They had to have it right away in self-defense. Given what he'd just heard, Rosie understood.

He looked around at the men who were sitting around him. As he did the guitarist strummed a single note with a dramatic flair. It seemed as though the sound sent a wave of hurt through the audience. They must have known what was coming. They were anticipating what the fado singer was going to do with this one.

One loud, piercing sound came out of her throat and seemed to hang in the atmosphere for an obscene length of time. It sent chills through Rosie's flesh. Damn, this woman wasn't going to let up at all!

The men squirmed in their chairs. They didn't seem to be able to look at one another. When the woman went on and began to move through the song, it seemed as though some communal guilt was gripping the tough fishermen and other workers who were gathered here.

Gotta be a song about doing a woman wrong, Rosie thought to himself. It was the only explanation he could find for the strange collective behavior of the males.

A loud noise broke through the tension at their table. It was that idiot Appelbaum. He slammed a new bottle of green wine down on the surface. It had been opened at the bar and the liquid splashed out onto the tabletop. "Damn good stuff, huh, Rosie?"

"Pipe down, you watery-eyed idiot," Rosie whispered. "You're going to get yourself killed. Can't you see that this is some kind of religion going on here? These guys will eat you for dinner if you don't stop interrupting the music."

"Damnation," Marty muttered as he filled his glass with the wine. "Can't have any fun anywhere." He emptied the drink in a single throw back of his head.

Not for the first time, Rosie wondered just how the man did it. It seemed as though the little guy could drink endless glasses of booze and never get drunk. He'd seen him snorting large amounts of Cowboy's cocaine without effect too.

There'd been one time that Cowboy and Rosie had tooted so much of the white powder that they'd stayed awake and alert for something like three days. But Marty, who, if anything, had done more of the stuff, simply announced it was his bedtime, went off, and was snoring within minutes.

It didn't really shock Rosie. Chemical imbalance was one of

the least ridiculous explanations for Appelbaum's personality. Whatever the cause, terminal assholism was certainly the result.

The woman's voice went into one of those piercing solos again, one of the ones where she did something that let her maintain a single high note for an inhuman length of time. It was a guarantee that it would make the men more morose. Rosie looked around and saw that some of them were crying again.

Rosie just hadn't seen so many tears falling from male eyes in his life. Not even a Southern funeral had this much crying going on. Whatever else these Latin males might have going for them, no matter how much they might get into their macho posturing, give them a bottle of green wine and a fado singer and they were going to start running the water like Niagara Falls.

Cowboy was obviously mesmerized by the song—or at least by the singer. Well, if he wanted her, he could have her. Rosie was interested, no doubt about that. But he would never, ever let a woman come between him and his buddies. That was the first lesson of building a team. It didn't even bother him if he was the one who got cut out of the sex action the most.

Sex was something that Rosie got more than enough of. There were plenty of dark-skinned women around the world who'd been more than happy to spread their legs and show him their nappy pubic hair and there'd be plenty more in his lifetime. He was sure of it.

Cowboy, that was a different story. The man *had* to have his piece. He just had to get it on, especially if the woman was Latin.

The fly-boy had been furious that their stop at Palermo was just a quick one. He had acted as though his mama had just told him that Santa Claus wasn't going to come that Christmas. But he was quickly cured when he found out that Oporto was the actual destination.

Seems he had some very fond and recent memories of a lady

down in Brazil. He kept blabbering about the sweet sound of her voice and the way the Portuguese language had added the seduction of French to the passion of Spanish.

Cowboy would find a way to get this singing lady or whoever else he wanted. When unleashed against the charms of a Latin woman, Cowboy would become so totally obsessed that it was impossible for him to be kept from his prize.

When Billy Leaps Beeker walked in and stood at the bar, Rosie immediately realized that the Black Berets' leader wasn't going to be looking for a little tonight. There was every indication he'd already had his fair share.

Rosie filled his glass and sat back in the chair while pretending to pay close attention to the fado singer, who was making this particular song go on and on. He was enjoying the wine. Might as well. As soon as Beeker understood how much they had had, their booze supply would be cut off. The damn half-breed was a damn moralist when it came to their behavior in the field—or in front of Tsali. You'd think they had signed up to join a Methodist camp meeting instead of a mercenary group.

Rosie looked back at Beeker, who was taking an inventory of the rest of the people in the bar. Yes, he definitely had gotten some from Delilah.

On another man you could tell that he'd just had sex because he'd be happy, he'd be in a good mood and want to crow a little bit to his pals. But not Beeker. Whenever Billy Leaps got laid you'd think that he'd just suffered some grievous injustice, that someone had taken something from him.

Rosie supposed that whenever a man like Beak had to admit that he wanted something special that could be given only on the whim of a single person, well, that took away some of his power. It made him weak somehow and showed just how vulnerable he was.

Beeker's whole life had been making himself strong and self-reliant. He could be a part of a team, all right, but only if he was the leader. Now, with a son and a woman, he had more baggage than he'd ever had in his whole existence before. And he had the weight that came with those things.

It couldn't be a happy life for Beeker. Not at all.

Beeker stood at the bar and drank a glass of mineral water while the singer went on with her sad tale. There was a man standing beside him who seemed to be the only other one in the room who wasn't hypnotized by her. He was leaning over the bar on his elbows, studying a glass of amber liquid. It looked to Beeker as though it was hard liquor, not the wine that most of the others were drinking.

The man looked as though he was Beeker's age, about thirty-eight. If they'd been back in the States, Beeker would have studied his complexion hard and wondered if the guy wasn't an Indian. The skin was tan enough and his eyes were dark enough for it to be so. But, no, he was Portuguese, Beeker was sure.

There was another thing about him that would have made Beeker question his background if they'd been back in America. He was wearing military-issue camouflage pants. They ballooned out a bit over his thighs and then tightened up around the heavy paratrooper boots he was wearing.

This bar wasn't the kind of place where the young kids were wearing military chic clothing. There was every probability the man was for real. That explained some other things that Beeker sensed about him.

He'd been in combat. Billy Leaps just knew it. There was something about the intensity with which he was studying the glass and the way his arms were crafted with ropy muscle that displayed tension as much as a good physique. Beeker looked beside the glass and saw that there was a deep purple beret there. It was obviously this guy's and he was sure it signified something that was just as important to him as Beeker's own black beret was to himself.

There was a story here. Billy Leaps wondered what it might be. But it wasn't his style to ask.

It was his style to notice that they were going to get some company. There were three other men whose attention had drifted from the fado singer and seemed to be directed toward the stranger at the bar. They were talking to one another in whispers. They thought they weren't being observed, as though their low voices could negate the obvious stares they were making at the drinking man.

Beak took another sip of his mineral water and thought about how stupid most people were. He wasn't looking back at the trio, but he was sensing them the way that any real soldier felt an enemy. They were untrained and they were inexperienced. But this other guy by him wasn't. Beeker knew that he was just as aware of the conspirators as he was.

Another round of applause overtook the bar. The men called out to the singer. The words were similar to those that any crowd might give to an entertainer—but there was a difference. They were honestly conveying the way the men in the bar were distraught over the idea of the woman taking a break and leaving them.

There was a sudden burst of louder music as the bartender turned on the jukebox. A lighter and faster-paced series of tango-like songs came screaming out of the speakers that had been jerry-rigged in the four corners of the large room.

There was a lot of movement all of a sudden. Men came to the bar for faster refills for their drinks; others were going to use the facilities; some leaving after the most recent set of the fado songs. The man beside Beeker was obviously one of those who'd decided to call it a night. He left his drink half full and walked out into the darkness. The three men who had been studying Beeker's silent neighbor started to move after him. They obviously had some plans.

Billy Leaps never did think about these things. It was just a reaction that he'd learned to trust when his guts told him something. Right now they were saying that this guy was all right. He was like Beeker in some way. There was some bond between them, even if just what it was had never been verbalized.

He was a pal. He was about to be attacked. He wasn't going to be left to fight these people alone.

Beeker hadn't really bothered to arm himself when he left the hotel room. They didn't even know who their enemy was yet. They hadn't made a move in Portugal and there was no need for them to be in any state of real alert.

But there was an eight-inch stainless-steel survival knife sheathed inside his right boot. He wore it all the time. It was something he carried out of instinct. He paid no more attention to it than he did to the socks he wore beside it. He walked out of the bar after the rest of them. As soon as he was outdoors Beeker bent down, moving so slowly that anyone looking on would just have thought that he was getting something up off the ground.

He didn't have to bother. Before he had even reached his boot there was a sudden *Thump!* He knew the sound. He moved more quickly to retrieve his knife, forgetting any attempt to cover his motion. But there was another *Thump!*

Beeker had the steel blade in his hand and was in a crouched fighting stance in a matter of maybe three seconds. When he looked up he saw that two of the men were on the brick sidewalk. The sound had been a knife blade striking the chest of each one and piercing them—mortally.

In the short time that it had taken Beeker to see the danger and start to make his move to get his knife, the unknown Portuguese had not only thrown his own two blades with deadly accuracy, he'd gotten across the alley and now held the third one's neck in his grip.

The target's face was already turning the telltale purple that said there wasn't enough oxygen getting past his throat to keep his brain functioning. His eyes were grotesquely popping out, as though the pressure being applied was so great that they were never going to survive if they didn't escape his skull.

The man was helplessly struggling with the death grip. He was in such a state of panic that he couldn't figure out the moves that might have saved him. All he could do was try to get the hands around his throat to stop.

Beeker stepped into the shadows. This wasn't some kind of simple assault. It wasn't a question of someone deciding to roll the guy. There was more going on here. The attack had clearly been planned. He had no intention of stopping his unnamed friend from taking his revenge. But he knew enough to suspect that there might be even more trouble coming his way. Billy Leaps decided he would be smarter if he waited here, just to see what might happen.

He held the stainless-steel blade in his hand. He would have liked to have a rifle right now, at least a decent pistol. Those Czech arms they'd used in Libya were suddenly much nicer in his memory than they had been during the operation. Still, he hardly felt defenseless with a survival knife like this. He had used the silent weapon so often that it felt like an extension of his own body right now.

There were some movements in the shadows behind the still-struggling pair. Beeker moved quickly toward them, clinging to the cover he himself had from the occasional streetlights.

He kept his back hard against the stone wall of the building. There was a surge of adrenaline, the chemical high he automatically got when he was ready for a battle.

He watched the darkness behind the fighters, looking for some outline that was even more black than the rest of the space. There was something. He saw a quick and minute reflection of light against some kind of metal. He moved toward it.

He was on peak, ready, his senses at highest alert. He tried to make out the sounds of the human being—or beings—that was moving toward him.

There was a sudden soft sound behind him. He knew that his friend had just finished off the job and had dropped the now dead body to the ground. He only hoped the Portuguese had been as observant as he'd been inside and understood that Beeker was an ally, not one of the assailants. He had to trust that right now. There was no choice.

There! Another small reflection. Beeker suddenly had a mental image of the one—he was sure there was just one—man who was armed and still approaching. Just from those small reflections and from the slightest hint of an outline, he could imagine how the man was standing, how he was moving, and at what speed.

There wasn't much time. He knew the man was getting ready to leap on the unsuspecting Portuguese. Billy Leaps Beeker made his final decision: The man would die before he had the opportunity.

Beeker lunged forward. His arm reached out. If he was right and his hunter's skill hadn't failed him, he would grab hold of the man's chest. He felt a hard body covered by cotton. There was a sudden jerk to the torso. It hadn't expected anything to come at it from this direction. Beeker's mind's eye continued its calculations. He held on to the man with all his strength, taking full advantage of his shock.

Beeker drew back his blade. He prayed a silent prayer to his father's spirit, and he plunged the knife into the man's chest. There was the all-too-familiar feel of steel cutting through skin, then scraping against bone, and finally the rush of blood.

There was a quick and loud scream. Beeker knew that sound as well. It was a death cry that had been heard on every battlefield in the world since men came together to fight common enemies—and to lose to them.

The yell was soon drowned out by a gurgle of liquid. The blood that had been freed from inside the man's lungs was forming a geyser that spewed out of his throat.

Beeker knew his wound had been fatal. He tossed the man down on the ground and stepped back; his knife blade was dripping blood on the ground.

There was a hand on his shoulder. Beeker knew what it was and stopped his natural reactions to attack the sudden force. "Quickly. This way."

There was the sound of a group of men coming out of the barroom nearby. They were headed in this direction. Beeker knew there wasn't any good reason for him to stay around and try to explain just how four corpses ended up here.

He followed the nameless man down the alley, both of them running as fast as they could.

9

"You speak good English."

The man looked at Beeker and smiled. "I went to Coimbra." Billy Leaps looked at him with an obvious questioning glance. "Our Harvard." The way the man said it—dripping with sarcasm—told Beak that he didn't have to worry. This guy wasn't one who would take that shit seriously.

They were in another *taverna* now. Beeker had his mineral water and the man who'd introduced himself as Filipe Covilha was sipping on another glass of scotch. Beeker tried not to pay too much attention to the whiskey. He didn't approve, but he reminded himself that this wasn't one of the Black Berets. His command didn't extend to Filipe's habits.

He felt strange about that. He sipped on his water and examined just how much he felt a kinship to this guy. There was the admiration that he felt for Filipe's ability to handle the three who'd mugged him.

"Where did you learn that?" Beeker suddenly spoke out. "How did you learn to handle knives?"

Filipe smiled. He reached into his belt and pulled out

another blade. It was six inches long and barely one inch wide. "In Mozambique they use these all the time. They've learned a lot there about knives. They know that a thick blade like yours is good for some kinds of hand-to-hand conflict. But a thin one like this goes into the body of an enemy more easily. If you trust yourself to know how to throw one, this is a deadly weapon.

"It's like guns, you know? If you are really good at it, you only need a .25, maybe even a .22, and you can work wonders. If you don't trust your aim, then you go higher. If you need them, you get bigger bullets to make up for your bad shot. Right? Isn't that the way it works?"

Beeker nodded. He knew the man was talking sense, he was clearly a seasoned veteran.

"But you don't know about Mozambique?"

"A little. It's in Africa. Portugal used to rule it. What else is there to know?"

Filipe smiled sardonically. "There, you see that?" He was pointing to a plain plaque that hung above the wall of the bar: 25 ABRIL 1974. "It's in every bistro and every drinking hall in the country. It's the day of our glorious revolution." He was obviously mocking the icon of liberty when he toasted it with a too grandiose manner.

"It was the day they shot us all in the back.

"Now, you have to understand, friend, I am not against the revolution. Caetano was a pig just like Salazar before him. They were reactionary fools who thought they could fight off all the trends toward modernization in the world, like that King Canute in England thought he could order back the tide.

"He had to go. But when he did, lots more went with him." Filipe picked up his nearly full glass of scotch and threw it down his throat in one quick movement. He slammed the glass on the bar and it was refilled quickly. He was obviously known here.

He was also obviously feared. Beeker could tell that by the way he got the fastest service and, at the same time, a total lack of friendliness from the saloon's workers.

"What went was the youth of all the young men of Portugal. We had fought for Mozambique and Angola, for Timor and Guinea. We left our best in those rotten jungles. We left our universities and our fishing villages, abandoned our sweethearts and our families, and we went fighting for the glory of Portugal!

"And then, on that day, the new government told us it had all been a mistake. The glory of Portugal had nothing to do with our being in Africa and Asia. We were suddenly 'oppressors' in the way of national 'self-determination.'" Filipe wasn't saying the words, he was spitting them out with all the sarcasm—and pain—that a grown man could display.

"Some of us couldn't tolerate that idea. We watched as the troops that had been fighting the guerrillas were ordered to hand over the keys to our cities to the new native regime. They were Communists. The very reason that generations of Portuguese men had given their lives and their youth had been to keep them out of power. But now those men's lives meant nothing.

"So we decided that the fight had to go on. We joined up with Renamo. But you don't know about Renamo, do you? Why should you know the history of a piece of insignificant swampland in southern Africa?"

The anger with which Filipe spoke betrayed how much he himself did care and how incredulous he'd been when he had actually discovered that he was one of the very few who did.

"The South Africans backed us. We were their first line against communism, they said. We were their allies in keeping Africa free. Those were good days, days when there were enough bullets to go on a patrol and enough food that you didn't starve to death.

"But even the damn Afrikaners have their price. They struck a deal with the Frelimo regime, which claimed to rule Mozambique. If the Reds would stop allowing South African dissidents to use Mozambique as a base, then the Afrikaners would stop supplying Renamo.

"Politics! Politicians! Governments! They know nothing about *men!*" Filipe stopped for a moment. "We were trapped, the last of the white Portuguese in Africa, without arms, without support, without anything that we could use to keep up a war. We left, finally realizing what fools we'd been to throw away our lives to people who would never honor our sacrifice.

"To the revolution!" With a last toast, Filipe polished off his scotch and once again had it refilled.

Beeker stood there and listened to the story with an increasing sense of disbelief and something even stronger. It was too much like Vietnam and the way Washington had handled it. There were too many similarities between the two events and the way that the men who had been sent to tropical lands had been treated.

Now he knew—all too well—why he had sensed a kinship with Filipe as soon as he'd seen him in the bar. He also knew why the clothing seemed so familiar. Filipe wore the remnants of his army uniform in the same way that so many Viet vets wore theirs. This had been the clothing that they'd worn during the most important days of their lives. Just because some politico in Washington—or Lisbon—said those days were over, and they hadn't really amounted to very much when they were taking place, didn't mean that the grunts in the field felt that way.

Beeker could just imagine what it must have been like to come back to Oporto from a place like Mozambique. They'd have gotten off the troopship, happy to be alive after having seen so much death, and they would have felt that they were the lucky ones, the survivors. They'd have been proud that they'd made it and they'd have been proud to have served their country.

But the welcoming party would have been made up of college brats who were now the "vanguard of the revolution" and fat bureaucrats who were rewriting history to tell the world that those campaigns in Africa had all been a terrible mistake, the actions of a misguided right-wing regime that was now discredited.

The veterans who'd given so much—and who'd seen even more—might have had memories of how other soldiers had returned home to a thankful country. But it wasn't going to be their fate this time. They were an embarrassment. They were the proof that there had been living, breathing Portuguese soldiers who'd been in those jungles, following their orders, for the common good and even the common glory.

But their heroism had to be rewritten with the rest of the country's history. That meant that they were advised to hide their past, not to talk about it. Please, don't remind the *turismos* about that chapter in our lives.

There probably were plenty of them who did just what Filipe was doing—they wore their uniforms as a protest, just the way the American vets did. They weren't going to let those wasted years be forgotten and they weren't going to play patsies to the idea of a revised history. They knew who was really to blame for their lack of pride and honor. The government.

It was so much like Nam . . .

The place they were standing was obviously one where the veterans of those campaigns hung out. There wasn't any live entertainment here, just a stereo playing ballads in a less emotional form than fado. The colors of dozens of outfits hung on the walls around the bar. Beeker couldn't make out the Portuguese words, but he didn't have to be able to read them to understand that they were the proof some poor soul had hung up to show he'd been one of them.

There were a couple of dozen other men in the bar who were as brooding as Filipe. They, too, wore pieces of old uniforms and talked in low, angry voices. There was no escaping their past. They knew that. And so did Beeker. He'd never escaped what Nam had been and what it had done to him. Why should these guys have a better break?

"And, so now?" he asked Filipe.

Covilha shrugged. "Now it's the new Portugal. Now it's industry and trade and many, many tourists. We're the cheapest country in Europe, friend Beeker. In so many ways we're the cheapest whore on the Continent. We will sell our women, our food, and our homes as cheaply as we sold our honor.

"Isn't that why you're here? To buy some of us? Aren't you one of the *turismos?*"

"No, not that. I'm a lot of things, Filipe, but I don't qualify as a tourist."

"Ah, then what, my friend, are you?" Covilha was obviously playing with him, and his teasing had an edge to it. Maybe he was so far into his scotch that he forgot that Beeker probably just saved his life a short while ago.

"I'm a soldier."

"Then you are definitely in the wrong country, friend Beeker. This isn't a place that likes soldiers, not at all." Filipe's smile went. "But I'm a man who knows a comrade when he sees one. And, besides, I'm someone who owes you a big favor. Those departed souls we left back in the alley had debts they wanted to collect from me. They weren't going to be satisfied with the few dollars I had in my pocket. They weren't after money—those aren't the kinds of debts we're talking about. So now I owe you. You're going to collect?"

Beeker stood and looked at the man. "I don't like doing that—cashing in my chips as soon as I've raked them in. But I think you could help me, and a lot of other people. There's a problem here. Maybe you already know about it?"

Beeker was making a big gamble. He was still just going on his instinct. There was no way they could find their way through a strange city like Oporto and even know what they were looking for. Delilah was pulling out the stops to get a new contingent of Washington sleuths into Portugal to try to pick up the pieces of the shattered CIA and Army Intelligence net-works. But those idiots probably wouldn't have been any good in any event, and even if they rose above the Neanderthal level of most Langley recruits, they would face the same problems the Black Berets did: They'd be new to the place.

Beeker needed a lot of information and a lot of ideas and he needed them fast. Covilha was his best bet. But first he had to feel him out some more. A man like Covilha was probably burned enough by his past to be available to the highest bidder. The way he talked, he'd be none too pleased with the new civil-ian government and might very possibly have been predisposed to helping some folks who were out to give it trouble.

Filipe shrugged and smiled. "There are many things that other people would consider problems, my friend. There's trade. There are women. It all depends on your definition. It's one thing the philosophy professors taught me at Coimbra."

Beeker stared Filipe in the eye. He wanted to make sure the soldier understood that the Black Beret was taking this all very seriously. "Do you know anything about people who'd want to fuck with NATO Intelligence—and the Soviets at the same time?" This was dangerous enough; there was no need to get into the bombs right away. He'd tell Covilha later on—if it seemed wise.

Filipe whistled. "You want awfully big favors, my friend. I'm not sure my miserable life is worth such enormous risks." He only sipped at his scotch this time. "What do you think? That I'm still doing freelance and would know things about spies? Cloak-and-dagger movies don't entertain me much. The real-life stuff is even less interesting. I haven't paid much attention to it recently."

Beeker picked up on the hint of a qualification. Covilha wasn't saying that he didn't pay attention to it, just not much. He knew this was a signal to press the Portuguese fighting man some more.

"I need to know who would want to come in and shut down the intelligence networks of every major power in Europe."

"Why?" Filipe was hardened now. He wasn't playing any more games.

"Because if I know that, then I'll know who has some things in his possession that I want to get my hands on."

"My friend, the people you want are not going to invite you to a garden party. They are some of the most brutal men in the world. They . . ."

But then Covilha broke into a smile. "You would need an army to get at them. Do you have one or are you recruiting?"

"You make it sound as though you'd be interested if I was," Beeker answered.

"I am bored, my friend. I am very bored. I live on a small amount of money from my family. It's one reason I'm here in Oporto and not in my native Lisbon. I'm paid to stay away and not embarrass them. And I have a small pension from the Army—another form of blackmail. But I have no action. I am not that old. I would have stayed and fought in Africa if there had been someone I could have tolerated. But the Afrikaners showed their real colors to me and my men. We left.

"A little action—if it wasn't suicidal, you understand—that would be interesting."

"It's more than that, isn't it?"

"Friend, I know who you want. I have my own debts to pay to him. If you are really going to act, then I have reasons to want to act with you. But are you alone? Are the two of us going to attempt this ourselves?"

"No. I have men here."

"I can get you more. Not many, but the best. They wore this with me in Mozambique." Covilha picked up his purple beret and seemed to stare blankly at it. No, Beeker realized, that was wrong. He was actually studying it reverently, as though that one part of his old uniform held all the tiny fragments of glory that still existed in it. He knew that feeling. His own black beret felt much the same to him.

He was going to get along awfully well with Filipe Covilha. Awfully well.

10

"I could blow it up easy."

"Why, in the name of God, would you want to do *that?*" Rosie asked.

As soon as he did Marty Appelbaum seemed to crumple up in a little ball. He was hurt that Rosie would talk to him that way. "After all, I am supposed to be a demolition expert."

Rosie stared at the little wimp as though he was some strange alien brought back from outer space. Try as hard as he could, he didn't understand the way the sick Jersey boy's head worked. He looked back at the beautiful steel bridge that spanned the Douro River. Why would Appelbaum . . .

"I figure I'll never have a chance to get the tower," Marty said wistfully. "At least I can have the bridge, that makes sense, doesn't it?"

Rosie shut his eyes in a futile attempt to defend himself against the ignorance of the world, so much of it personified in this bleary-eyed blond man in front of him. Of course he should have realized how Marty's feeble mind would work in a matter like this.

The bridge they were talking about had been built by A. G. Eiffel, the same man who'd constructed the world-famous tower in Paris. A fool like Appelbaum—all of whose dreams were built around destruction—must have spent countless hours fantasizing about the glory of tearing apart one of the world's most famous structures. It would be his most fond thought. *The day I blew up the Eiffel Tower.* But even Appelbaum must have some idea that the idea was impossible. He'd have to find a substitute.

He probably came in his pants when he realized that the architect had designed another, less well-known steel structure. Here it was, soaring over a small river in a second-class European city—not even a capital—and there wouldn't be much notice if it was bent up a little.

Rosie shook his head and opened his eyes. Every once in a while he had to dig deep into his mind and come up with some way to communicate with Appelbaum in a manner that would make sense to his warped intellect. He thought he had it.

"Marty, no one would notice. They'd just think it was an accident or maybe a leftist guerrilla. It wouldn't do you any good." That was it! Appelbaum, after all, was an artist with his explosives. A true artist has to have an audience for his work to be appreciated. Take away the applause and . . .

It worked. The little man crumbled up some more; all of his dreams had just evaporated. "You're right," he admitted. "I can't do it."

Rosie smiled and looked at all the passersby and realized that all of them were going to keep on being able to cross the river on that nice steel bridge because of what he'd done for them. Too bad, he had the same dilemma as Marty. No one would ever know what an artist he was.

He drank some more of the thick coffee. This was powerful shit. He knew that the Portuguese had developed a taste for the real thing back in the days when they'd owned Brazil and the plantations that happened to come with it. They liked their brew dark and they liked it rich, there was no doubt about that. Just the way that Cowboy liked his ladies. Rosie looked at his watch. Where was that man, anyhow?

Cowboy had ducked out with the singing *senhorita* last night and they hadn't heard from him since. He was supposed to meet them here, in the central plaza of the city, an hour ago. Well, Rosie thought, if he's not here, they'd just have to start without him. Not that it was such a big deal. They had almost nothing to go on. They were just going to make like tourists and keep their eyes open. For what? Who knew. Maybe some helpful fellow would put out a flag: FIVE ATOMIC BOMBS ON DISPLAY. RIGHT THIS WAY! What a fucked-up way to earn a living.

The blond pilot was actually sprawled across the satin sheets of a lovely lady named Beatriz Vieira. He let the sounds roll off his tongue. It was a beautiful name for a beautiful woman who had a beautiful voice. He stretched against the satin and let its cool embrace give him a hint that maybe—just maybe— he might have the superhuman ability to do it again. After last night, who knew?

He reached for his lady friend and found only empty space. "Hey, Bea, honey," he called out. But there was no answer. He got up and wrapped one of the sheets around his waist. Daylight was one thing that Cowboy had a great deal of difficulty with. He couldn't stand to have the sun's full rays strike against his eyes. He groped on the table and found his shades. He put them on and, properly attired as far as he was concerned, started to search for Beatriz.

He roamed through the old but elegantly maintained apartment calling out her name. The place was so big he wondered if she was a real star. She certainly had some money from some place to live in this fashion. When he finally found her she wasn't acting like a grand lady. She was standing in the kitchen, hard at work at an omelet. He could smell the spicy sausage and perky herbs that were part of it.

More important, he could see Beatriz's fine ripe hips and he remembered the way they felt when his hands had held on to them while . . . No, there was no doubt about it now. He could *definitely* consider doing it again. At least once more.

He moved up behind her and put his hands on her waist. There was nothing on underneath her shift. That very thought made the possible turn into the necessary. He moved closer, letting his obvious physical need make its message known.

But in the time-honored fashion of so many other Latin ladies, Beatriz wasn't going to be deferred from her real task. "None of that!" she admonished him. "You have to eat. You're much too thin."

"You don't like me?" Cowboy asked with a mixture of real hurt and real fear in his voice.

"Oh, my little cowboy." Beatriz turned and put her arms around his shoulders. "You are the most wonderful lover a woman could ever have and the most handsome with all your golden hair all over your body." She giggled. "*All* over it. But that doesn't mean that you shouldn't eat more. You must!"

Actually, one of the many reasons that Cowboy loved Latin women was their intense maternal drive. They'd see him and they'd see an empty vessel that needed to be filled with the best in rice, bean, and meat dishes as much as they would want something else to fill themselves. He adored the attention and the way it allowed him to regress into a childhood he never had.

He obediently sat at the kitchen table with the satin sheet tied around his waist and waited. Beatriz had made coffee and, while the omelet finished cooking, she poured him a cup. Then she gave him a roll, homemade and bursting with cinnamon.

He ate to his heart's content. The meal was almost as good as sex—at least a barely acceptable substitute. But that didn't mean he was willing to accept just the second best. That wasn't his way.

The glasses were part of his secret. He honestly wore them because the sun did hurt his eyes. But he'd learned that women went crazy when they studied the reflecting lenses. They were convinced that he was studying them behind that protection.

They never ceased to amaze him. There he'd be, just eating a breakfast like this one with a woman like Beatriz across the table from him, and they'd look into his eyes. They acted as though they were two matching black canvases. While he was doing nothing more than eating his meal, they'd convince themselves that he was actually undressing them with his stares. While he was doing nothing more than watching his fork move through the omelet, they would believe that he was actually ready to leap across the table at them.

It was almost as though they wanted that to be the truth. It didn't make any difference if, like Beatriz, they were hoping it was true or, like some libber back in the States, they thought that he was some animal for even daring to think that they'd let him do a thing like *that*. Leave a woman alone with Cowboy while he was wearing his glasses and in a matter of minutes she'd be convinced that she was powerless to stop him.

A woman would persuade herself that she could either give in to her own desires and help along the seduction, or else give in to the violent assault that this man was sure to make on her. That's what the pilot did to the entire female sex. It was as predictable as . . .

Beatriz was moving now. She left her seat at the table and

went behind his chair. He was still chewing on a piece of sausage when he felt her hands on his naked back.

"No, Cowboy, I must go to work."

He shrugged. He figured he'd be able to see her again later in the day and he was already late to meet the rest of the guys. "Okay."

"Please, don't do this."

"Huh?"

"Don't make me so irresponsible." She leaned down and planted a kiss on the back of his neck. "I must go or else my brother will be very angry." Her hands reached around to the front of his chest and moved down the surface, over his belly. She had to be kneeling, she was pushing against the sheet now, forcing it down.

Cowboy put his fork on the plate; he was finished. But Beatriz was just starting. "No, Cowboy, I must go, stop doing this to me." He only sighed. He wasn't doing a thing, but her hands were doing plenty. There was no way he'd be able to get back to the bed with the sheet hanging around his waist now. It was too late.

But she'd made her point. He turned around in the chair. She was on her knees. He moved, as though to join her on the floor. He loved to just *have* sex. To just *do* it. There was a surge of excitement in him over the idea of taking her on the floor.

But her own arousal wasn't giving him much room to make the decisions between them. "I get you, Cowboy, stop it and don't make me . . . I must go to work." With that she shifted, still on her knees and her mouth opened. There was no question what she intended to do.

Cowboy just looked down at her and braced himself for the sensation that he knew was coming any minute now. He closed his eyes in anticipation. But Beatriz didn't know that. She was still filling in the blanks that she saw in his mirrored glasses. "Don't make me do this . . ."

Cowboy only felt wet warmth engulfing him. He leaned back in his chair and let out a small guttural cry. Whatever else was going to happen, he wasn't going to make Beatriz do anything she didn't want to.

"Hurry, you beast. Look! You've made me late." Cowboy only smiled as Beatriz ran through her bedroom pulling clothes out of her dresser drawers and yanking others from her closet.

He wasn't going to argue with her. If she wanted to make believe he'd coerced her into anything, that was fine with him. He was still warm and glowing from their little encounter among the herbs and spices of the kitchen.

He loved this moment almost as well. There didn't seem to be anything more intimate than watching a female put on her underwear. As Beatriz pulled up her panties Cowboy studied the immodest display and felt something deep and elemental happening to him. This is what a man did when he lived with his wife. He'd see her putting on her panties, fitting her breasts into the cups of her bra. All of it.

It was the beginning of the end. And, even if it was as predictable as the sun rising in the sky, Cowboy never could recognize it for what it was: He was falling again.

Cowboy never did just fall in love. That's different. Rosie might do that. Even Harry was capable. And whatever it was that Beeker did with Delilah might have something to do with that normal human process. Cowboy did something different. Cowboy fell into wanting to get married.

It was especially true after sex with a beautiful Latin lady, and even more after watching her get dressed in the morning. It was a good thing that Beatriz couldn't see his eyes behind his shades when she stood up now and pulled on her skirt. If she had, she would have been making plans for her first trip to the altar at that very moment. There was no doubt at all what that expression meant. None in the least.

"Do you have to go?" he asked her dreamily.

"Of course, Cowboy. My brother would never stand for a lack of discipline. He's a great man. Or he was before the Socialists took over and began to undermine the resolve of the Portuguese people." She was finished dressing. She stood and looked at Cowboy. "We were once the rulers of the seas, Cowboy. Alfonso means to make us great again."

"I think you're great just the way you are, Beatriz." He meant it. His mind wasn't working in any logical way right now. The words about her family were just moving through his ears and having no effect except telling him that this beautiful woman—who would look so good in a long white dress with a lace veil to go with it—was going to leave him.

It hurt. It hurt terribly to know that she was going to abandon him. After that good meal and the careful way she'd paid such loving attention to his body, how could she just leave? Vague thoughts were coalescing in his mind. Somehow they included the idea that if she were married to him, she wouldn't be going off.

"When are you coming home, baby?" He didn't ask it as though it were a normal question. It was more a plea. It expressed all the pain he was feeling as he contemplated being so far away from this beautiful woman for even a few hours.

"Oh, my Cowboy, I'll be home tonight. You'll come by, won't you? We can go out, to the nightclubs."

Cowboy was struck by a sudden wave of emotion. "Oh, no, honey. Let's just stay home, like regular people." *Like regular married people* is what he meant to say.

"Of course, Cowboy, if that's what you want." Then she kissed him on the cheek and took his hand. "But now we have to go. I must get to work. Come, I'll give you a ride in my new car. It's a Lancia. Much too much of an expense"—she tried to affect an adult voice—"but after all, I must drive so far to get there every day. It's only right that a woman in my position travel in comfort and style."

At the end her voice sounded more like a little girl trying to explain to Daddy just why she *had* to have a new dress. But Cowboy didn't mind. He was just trying to figure out what color it should be.

11

"What if she finds me?" Cowboy cried to Beeker. "She'll think I was lying when I said I'd meet her. It's the same bar where she sang."

"You were lying," the Black Berets' leader said.

"You made me do it."

"I didn't do a damn thing to make you go out and try to get yourself married again. You damned fool, can't you even look at a woman and not want to go out and buy a gold ring?"

"Sure he can," Rosie laughed. "Just introduce him to a Dane and you'll get to see an ice storm. A good blond Scandinavian woman wouldn't do a thing for him."

Neither Beeker nor Cowboy laughed along at the joke. Billy Leaps closed the subject: "We're on assignment. You keep your pecker in your pants for once. We have a job to do and you know damn well how important it is. Now we have some help with Filipe and we're going to have to take as much advantage of it as we can while we can. There's nothing else to go on in this city right now. So shape up, Cowboy.

"And the rest of you too." Beeker swept the room with his

gaze to let them all realize that he was deadly serious about this. "You're in for a surprise. While you were all sitting around guzzling your booze—"

"A little wine, Beak." Rosie defended them against the verbal assault. But he should have known it wouldn't do any good.

"A flood of the stuff. Alcohol is alcohol. You people can pickle your livers when you're not on assignment and not on the farm, but right now you're under the strictest discipline you've ever known. We have a potential atomic disaster somewhere in this country and I won't have you all half snockered while we try to avert it."

Harry clamped a hand on Marty's shoulder as a silent order to him not to argue with Beeker right now. Not when the Black Beret leader was in this kind of mood. It simply wasn't worth it to even try.

They'd eaten a simple meal at their hotel—without so much as a glass of wine. Now it was time to begin the new part of their operation. But there were some accessories that they were going to need.

Filipe might like his slender blades, but the nighttime work the Black Berets might be doing called for something more substantial. They'd gotten survival knives from a camping store. The six-inch blades were designed with a 23-degree convex arc that provided enough curve to increase their cutting power. There'd be less problem tearing the razor-sharp blade through flesh because there was less drag. The oval-shaped handle was covered with a new rubber compound, Creton, that gave them a superior gripping surface.

There was something else extra-good about the blade. The handle was topped by a brass protrusion—a skull crusher. The top was pointed enough that when the hard metal was slammed into a human head, it could pulverize the bones and kill a man as swiftly as the blade itself. It wasn't quite a two-ended knife— but it was damn close.

The men would have liked to put on their full uniforms. But that would have caused too much notice. For now each one chose some part of it as a piece of his outfit. Cowboy wore the camouflage shirt; Harry, the boots; Beeker, the beret; Marty, the pants. They each could touch that one part of his uniform and know that it was happening—they were going out into the field. Later, when it was necessary, they'd put on the whole thing. But for now, beginning their serious undercover work, this was the start of it and the individual pieces were their totems.

Rosie was the only one who didn't have on a piece of clothing. Appelbaum looked at him crossly with a silent communication that something was wrong. The big black man grinned and went over to stand in front of the mirror over the dresser. He reached into his pocket and pulled out his earring.

It was a piece of Rosie, something that multiplied the already frightening vision of his physical presence. He finished putting the ring through his earlobe and turned. He laughed out loud—it was a little too much like the laugh of a madman.

The earring was a small skull. It was a piece of great craftsmanship. Every detail was accurate, as though it hadn't really been styled but had been created by an obscene shrinking of a real human head. More than a few people had looked at it and then into the eyes of Roosevelt Boone and had to wonder if that wasn't the truth. They might know—intellectually—that it was impossible for it to be so, it was simply too small. But when they studied it against the ebony skin of the huge man and felt the primal sense of him, that aspect of his personality that let them know that he really was descended from the great warriors of Africa, then the idea that the small ivory piece dangling from his ear was real was something they had to take into consideration.

They were going to need handguns. Delilah had arranged for all the weapons they'd need. They didn't ask her how she did it. They knew better than that. Over in the closet there was a collection of M-16s and M-60s with enough ammunition for a NATO war game. But they couldn't walk the streets of the city with that kind of firepower. They had needed something more subtle.

She'd collected accurized Colt Officer's .45s for them. The cut-down .45s were the latest from the venerable American firearms company. Until the Officer's Colts came along, you had to take a .45 into a gunsmith if you wanted him to cut down the length of the barrel. But now, with new technology, the Colts were easily hidden in the shoulder or waist holsters that the men wore. They weren't even seven inches in length and were less than five inches high. They had a blue matte finish that kept them from reflecting light and made them especially handy at night.

They were ready. They would have liked more. Those M-16s, cammy grease on their faces, their complete uniforms, all of it. This was a tease. Getting ready, but only with a knife and a handgun. Being dressed, but only in parts. Going into the field, but only to reconnoiter. They wanted more.

The fact of preparation and the idea that there might be any kind of real action changed them enough as it was, though. They walked out of their hotel quietly. People who watched them were aware that this group of large men made almost no noise. They moved gracefully, as though any step they made might have landed on a mine. They were all-observant. But their sight was as a group, not as individuals.

The five of them moved in a diamond. Beeker was in the middle. Protect your leader, rule number one. Make sure the one who knows what's going on isn't the one who's at risk.

As they walked down the streets of Oporto toward the bar where they were going to meet Filipe, Rosie led the way. Even if it was a city in Europe, even if this was the time of night when the place was packed with tourists and with office workers and secretaries on their way to dinner or a movie, Rosie's position was still the same thing as being on point. There was no other way to put it.

He was the one who was looking straight ahead and watching for anyone who'd move directly toward them and who looked like he might be dangerous. If the attack came from there, then he'd be the first one to take the heat. It came with the territory.

Cowboy and Marty took the flanks. They ignored everything in front of them—that was Rosie's. Instead, they each watched the sides of the group, making sure that there was no movement from an alley, no sudden appearance of an unknown person from a shop entrance. That was theirs, their responsibility.

Harry brought up the rear. He moved in subtle ways that allowed him to catch a backward glance whenever possible. He was the one with his back to the unknown. He was the one who could get it with the least warning.

They moved to the run-down area of town toward the *taverna*. When they arrived they entered single file. Rosie was already sitting down on a stool by the time Harry walked in. To the rest of the world it looked just as though they were a group of guys who were out for a drink. That's all. Just a friendly bunch of fellows who might toss one back together. But any witness who would have known what to look for would have seen something else. He would have seen a military operation carried out with such intricate planning that it was invisible to the rest of the world.

They were pros.

Filipe moved toward Beeker when the Black Berets had settled down with a line of glasses filled with mineral water and fruit juices. He nodded to Billy Leaps to have him come and join him at his table. Beak stood up and went over to where Filipe introduced him to three other men.

Tomas Pombal, Luís Bonifacio, and Góis Almeida all carried the same indescribable air about them that the Black Berets had. They'd been there. They'd seen it. They knew what it was all about.

They were all about the same age, all in their late thirties. They all had faces that looked older than they probably were and bodies that were in much better shape. There wasn't a pound of excess fat on one of them. They must have stayed in training.

It made sense. Beeker had learned that Portugal was one of the great mercenary markets in the world. There were more disenchanted and experienced fighting men here than just about any other place, certainly in Europe.

The Portuguese weren't criminals. They could—as a national group—have moved against the Mafia if they'd wanted to. They could even have gone against the more vicious Corsicans. But it wasn't their style. They left the Italians alone when it came to organized crime. They had never challenged the Turks and the French as thieves. Beak wondered if there were many banks or museums in Europe that could stand up to an assault from a crack team of Portuguese military veterans. Probably not.

That wasn't their style. They were soldiers. They were professionals. They could be bought, but only to fight, not to steal and not to cheat. They would hate that. Instead, they were the best hired guns in the world. Give them a military objective, and it was yours. Ask them to attempt the impossible assault, and it was done.

Like real soldiers the world over, they'd been lied to, cheated, and misled by the best of them. Not just the South Africans that Filipe had told Beeker about. They'd gone to the limit with the Rhodesians; they'd taken arms from the Israelis; they'd been willing to make raids against the Indians. Give them a fight, they'd take the offer.

Now they were studying him and wondering just what this

American Indian wanted from them. They were wondering if it was worth risking their lives to follow him. He had one big thing to offer—to a group of guys like this, a fight with honor would be like a drink of spring water in the desert.

Beak looked from one to the other after he'd sat down, and he could even find the parallels between each one of them and the members of his own team. Beeker kept on studying them, trying to figure out each individual.

Tomas was jumpy. He'd been wounded in some campaign; there was a deep and angry red scar that ran from his cheekbone down under his jaw. He would keep on fingering it unconsciously, as though he needed to remind himself that it was there. Not that he was likely to forget that it had happened, but to touch that part of him that was his proof of his time in battle.

Beeker couldn't help but reach up and touch his own ear. The lobe had been shot off in Nam when a green grunt had freaked out. Billy Leaps had been carrying Rosie back behind American lines during the worst of Khe Sanh when it had happened. It was a joke—sort of—that the two of them had survived Charlie intact only to get Beeker blown up and nearly killed by some joker who'd had no experience and who made up for it by being trigger-happy.

Luís Bonifacio wasn't like that. There wasn't a single jumpy movement he made that Beeker would ever see. He had that depth to him, the same kind that Harry had. There was sadness and there was even pain, but there were no physical scars. Billy Leaps just understood that neither he nor Tomas would ever change places with the man. Their scars were things that you could see and they even had their utility. It was amazing how frightened people could get of a scarred man. But Luís had gone through something much more permanent even than a facial mark. You could tell. Just the way you could tell with Harry.

Góis Almeida was like Appelbaum. Maybe—hopefully—he hadn't been born this way, like Marty. Maybe the colonial wars the group of them had been through had changed him. Now he was gung ho to the max, ready to take anyone on. As soon as Beeker had sat down Góis began by asking where the "hit" was. He'd been watching too many American military movies, that was for sure.

The expressions on the other Portuguese men's faces proved to Beeker that they held Góis in the same disdain that the Black Berets kept Marty. That told him something. It let him know that they had to damn well respect the guy's ability in the field if they were going to put up with him. He'd remember that.

"I've given them some information," Filipe finally said. "But it's up to you to fill us all in some more."

"Who are you? How do you know one another?"

Filipe smiled. It wasn't an unpleasant grin. He didn't mean to indicate that he regretted knowing these men, but it wasn't any indication of joy, either. "Mozambique. We all stayed behind to fight with Renamo. We all nearly got killed. We all got out. We were the only ones that did." He shrugged.

There was an epic behind his simple words. But the world wouldn't want to hear it. Even more, Filipe didn't even want to tell Beeker. Billy Leaps understood. There were things that had happened to him and the rest of them in Nam that he never wanted to describe to anyone in his life.

It wasn't just that they were intimate stories that only a single loved one should hear. They were more than that. They were the most personal things about himself that told the world that there were parts of him missing. It was enough that the world saw his ear and Luís's scar. They didn't have to know about the ones that cut deeper than flesh.

Beeker nodded. "I'm glad to know you were together. That means you can still fight with one another."

No one argued with him.

"I need information. It's like this. Someone took out all the spies in Portugal for a short period of time. There was no rhyme or reason to it. They took them out—*all* of them—and there's been no move to keep them from being replaced. Whoever did it only wanted to make sure that something wasn't seen by eyes that would recognize what was there.

"I think I know what that something was. I have to get it back."

"Why?" Tomas asked. He was sipping on a glass of liqueur.

Beeker studied him. He was back to trusting his gut. These guys had to be in on all of it. "Because we're not talking about people who are interested in a good firefight or who are going to just mess up some banks or steal a little bit of spending money. They have atomic bombs."

A couple of whistles sounded, low and sincere. This was news that the Portuguese had to pay attention to.

"Who did it?" Góis asked.

"The only lead I have is something called the 'Lusitanian Liberation Front.' Do you know what it is?"

"No," Filipe answered for all of them. "But there have been many groups formed since the revolution. Once the dictators went, then anyone whose mother and father would vote for him could start his own party. But a Lusitanian Liberation Front— no, that's one that's new to me."

"Me too," Góis said. But he was obviously puzzling over something else. "The name makes it sound leftist. But the Socialists are in power here. They control it all already—and they are violently antinuclear. It's one of the big issues in politics— whether or not to let NATO keep atomic weapons on our soil. They wouldn't—"

"No, they wouldn't have to," Beeker said. He took a breath.

There was no good reason to give these men only half the information. "The name doesn't have to mean anything. But somehow these guys are tied up with the Palestinians under al-Kaldi. We know that. And they've had help from Qadhafi."

"That means nothing," Luís waved in the air. "Those people would help anyone who was opposed to any sitting government. They are pure and simple anarchists in a profound way, their politics are nothing."

"I agree. Qadhafi and al-Kaldi don't have to have political purity if they know that someone is out to cause disruption—especially of the West and anyone who's had anything to do with being against Israel."

"*Vieira!*" Tomas yelled. "Of course, Vieira."

"Don't be a fool. That old man is living in the Dark Ages," Góis answered.

"The Dark Ages where Jews are hated and despised," Tomas insisted. "And think—think about the idea of anarchy. He's gotten so much crazier that he's close to believing that it's the only way for things to work out."

"Do you think he'd be foolish enough to play with atomic weapons?" Góis said. But his tone of voice had changed. It was obvious to Beeker that Góis was taking this new idea very seriously.

"He'd do anything he could to overcome the current regime," Tomas responded.

"Who is this guy?" Beeker demanded.

Filipe lifted his glass and studied it. He took a minute to collect his thoughts before he spoke. "Portugal is nothing these days, friend Beeker. But remember, we were once the greatest colonial power in the world. It's hard to accept being nothing when you were once the best there was.

"This man, Alfonso Vieira, is a merchant. He's one of the

biggest in Oporto, just about the only really large merchant outside of Lisbon. He was one of the staunchest supporters of the Salazar regime, but with a difference. It was a difference that saved him when the old man got sick and his lacky Caetano took over and was finally toppled.

"Vieira thought that Salazar was too soft. He thought he had no philosophy. If Vieira had his way, Portugal would have tossed aside its traditional alliance with Great Britain and joined the Nazis in the war. He was very taken with the Final Solution. Because Salazar was—in the end—just a minor dictator, Vieira never joined his party, never really took part in his regime.

"He used to dream of the toppling of Salazar, just never loudly enough that the dictator came after him. But his revolution wasn't going to be a Socialist one. It was going to be one from the right that was going to make Portugal back into a world power.

"He still dreams of that. He runs his trading empire from an old castle not far from here. He has all the most modern equipment—computers and satellite hookups, all that money can buy.

"We know him because he's come to us. He's a little in love with us. Not that way—he's not queer. But he thinks that we're the legacy of Portugal's greatness. He can be very seductive to people who are veterans of the colonial wars. After so much hatred and so much disdain being heaped on the 'returning heroes,' there was suddenly a very rich man who would invite us to his fancy house and offer us his best wine and drink to be able to listen to our war stories.

"He's tried, in the past, to hire some of us. The details were always mysterious and they were always murky. But there was money offered, and he clearly had it. There was also adventure—we had had enough."

"But there might be others . . ." Beeker started to say. He

knew all about the ones back in the States who were willing to buy into those armchair dreams.

"Yes, there were others." Filipe looked at the other three men. There was some silent communication among them as they debated whether to let the American Indian know some secret. "He's just recently hired at least twelve men from the area, all of them veterans. They're 'bodyguards,' but he doesn't need that many. When did this thing happen? The interference with the agents?"

"Not long ago. Only two weeks or so."

"They would have been ready," Filipe said. "They would have had a month to prepare—"

"Where does this man live?"

"In the foothills of the Trás-os-Montes, the mountains that make the border with Spain. It's an ancient castle. They claim that even the Moors couldn't take the original structure centuries ago. It's one of the reasons that Vieira loves it so much. It was—according to legend—the place where Portuguese Christianity held out against the Islamic hordes."

"Will you go there with me?"

"Why?" Filipe asked. It was a point-blank question. "What could there possibly be in it for us?"

"What do you want? Money?"

Filipe thought for a moment. "We all have bills . . ." but just the way he spoke the words told Beeker that that was the least of their concerns.

"There'll be enough to take care of them and maybe a good fight for a decent cause added for extra measure."

Filipe smiled. "Oporto can be very boring."

They'd go.

12

This was more like it!

Rosie reached up and ran a hand over his newly shaven skull. It was his own sign that there was going to be real action. He demanded it. Tradition insisted upon it. When they went into battle Rosie went to one of the others with a straight-edged razor and made his companion shave him slick.

Where did it begin? He didn't honestly know. He just knew it was the thing that he needed. It was his transition. That's the only way to put it. When a man knew he was going to go out into the field, then he had to do something that would allow him to alter his personality, to change the very core of himself.

He had to get rid of any semblance of civilization. That was the best way to put it. He had to do something to take away the parts of him that had been taught to be too careful and to be too concerned and compassionate. Battle has no compassion. Not real battle. When you go out onto the field and you have an M-16 in your hands and the other dude has a rifle like it, then you don't worry about the etiquette of it all. You learn to get rid of that baggage that makes you wonder about taking a human life or risking your own.

That's what the shaving did. It was his symbol that he was scraping away that part of himself that would keep him from becoming a warrior.

Warrior. It was a good word. It was Beeker's. He wouldn't let them just talk about being soldiers. He wanted them to be part of a whole continuum of history. He wanted them to get back into some primal place where all the fighting men of the world had been—at least the ones that won, or at least the ones that survived.

It was the same for the others when they put on their clothes. Rosie wondered sometimes what he was like when that straight-edged razor was sliding across his black head. He wondered—if only vaguely—what changes came over his face and how his muscles moved. It had to be something like the others when they got dressed.

Because, of course, the Black Berets never "got dressed." They went through a metamorphosis. Their entire personalities moved through changes that humans aren't supposed to make.

He'd seen it earlier. They'd left the *taverna* as soon as Beeker was done with those Portuguese guys. They had information and it meant that they were going to move—now. The Black Berets had gone to their hotel room and they'd packed up. But first they had to get ready.

That's when Rosie had gone and gotten the razor and gone over and knelt in front of Beeker. He had been the supplicant asking for the priest's blessing. He'd gotten it with the swipes of the steel against his flesh.

When it was over he stood and started to get out his uniform. The others were farther along in their dress. But there was still the opportunity to watch them as they went through it— that dreaded and wonderful robing of the uniforms.

Cowboy had finished first. He'd taken his beret and gone and stood in front of the mirror. He'd taken both hands and lifted the small cap to his head. Then he'd put it on with a decisive motion, pulling it down hard, as though they were going to go out into a whirlwind and he might lose it. He wouldn't. It was attached by something a lot stronger than cloth.

Marty was next. He was just finishing buttoning his shirt. Sometimes Rosie wondered what each man thought about that camouflage material that masked his humanity. It meant something different for each of them. That was for sure.

For Marty it was his manhood. It was the one thing in this world that marked him as a member of a group. He was the one who'd never have anything in this life that meant as much to him as being a Black Beret. He was cocky when he put on the last touches of his clothing.

Harry was buttoning his shirt with an air of resignation. It seemed that the Greek simply expected all of this to be a part of his life. There was no excitement to it and there was no thrill. It was just there.

And, of course, there was Beeker. Rosie had looked up at the leader while he put on his beret. That was the strangest transformation of them all. Because there was no change. There was just Billy Leaps. It was the Marine in him, the part of him that thought a uniform was more normal than being buck naked. It was the stuff that his daddy and his DI and, most of all, his full-blooded grandmother had beaten into him from the minute they each got a hand on him.

To be out of uniform was to be deviant, something worse than anything else in the world. To be wearing civilian clothes meant that you weren't living life. You were only sleepwalking through your existence.

But what about himself? Rosie looked at the mirror and

saw his black, black face and his small white earring hanging down and he smiled. This was him. This was the time and place that he felt the most power and the most energy and the most reason for being alive.

They were going into the field. What a bullshit way to live. It was if he thought about it, in any event. But he seldom did. Every once in a while he'd think about some cottage on the Gulf Coast with a willing woman—or two—or more—and he'd wonder if that wouldn't be a better life. Give him some booze and have Cowboy come by with some blow every once in a while to make sure those gray cells of his could still see God, if only in a white haze, and it might be a decent life.

But he'd tried it. It didn't work. What worked was getting the action that meant his head was shaved, his uniform was put on, and his hands held a rifle that stunk of the same grease of every firearm in the world. This was life—at least for him.

There was no reason to wonder what that meant. All you could do with something like that is live it.

It took only about an hour for them to make their way toward the Trás-os-Montes. Cowboy drove the rented station wagon, following Filipe's lead. The highways weren't that bad until the very end. Then they got so difficult that they all instinctively knew that there was probably a reason for the sudden drop in surface quality. They were on a hilly slope that someone didn't want casual passersby to feel welcome driving on.

Filipe turned off into a grove of olive trees. Cowboy followed. They were obviously going to dump the cars here. The men got out and the two groups faced one another.

The Portuguese had gone through their own transformations. It was just the same thing. There was no way to look at it differently. They all had purple berets on their heads now.

They, too, had on complete uniforms. Theirs were older than the Black Berets, who understood that they must have been the authentic stuff from the Portuguese colonial army.

Rosie watched. He wondered if they would . . .

Yeah, they did. He leaned back against an olive tree and crossed his arms. He didn't need to take part in this one segment of the ritual. His face was naturally camouflaged. But the rest of them had to do something to make sure that the bright moon that was out wouldn't bounce off their white skin.

This was the chance to solidify the two groups and they were obviously going to take it. He watched while Beeker and Filipe approached one another. Each had a small can in his hand. They opened them and then the two men used their fingers to paint each other's face with the cammy grease. The others formed pairs and did the same.

Because they were so unqualifiedly male, because they probably would touch only their sons, maybe their fathers, perhaps their brothers, this way, the act of applying the cammy was made even more sacred.

Just as they would trust each other to save their lives, so they would allow a hand to caress a face. *Heavy.* That was the only word that flashed through Rosie's mind.

When the rite was over they all knew that it was time to move. All the Portuguese had been to the castle before. They all knew the grounds at least a little bit. They would have to be in charge.

Rosie and Beeker were going to follow Filipe. They were the point men, the first ones to approach, and—if there was an assault—they'd be the ones who saw the first action. Cowboy and Tomas were going far to the right. They were going to cover the assault group if it was necessary. From the other flank, Harry and Luís would do the same.

All of them held the M-16s in their hands. They all had knives in their belts and the pistols were still in holsters—though now they weren't bothering to hide them. They were more interested in quick access than they were in secret firearms.

Marty Appelbaum had one of his beloved M-60s. How the little man was able to carry the huge automatic rifle was one of the many secrets of life that Rosie would never understand. It was such an act of adoration for Marty that he probably wouldn't ever have felt the weight, that was the only reason. He must be like some of those Catholic fanatics who carry huge crosses up mountains to the shrines of their saints. They were in such ecstasy that they simply didn't even notice the size of the load. That was what it must be.

And if it was true of Appelbaum, it was the same thing with Góis Almeida. He was by far the smallest of the Portuguese, barely larger than Marty. But it turned out that he, too, had a passion for the M-60. The two men had been a little competitive at first, just the way two men after the same woman would have acted toward one another. But they'd gotten over that. They'd decided to share, at least this time around.

They were the heavy guns. They were the ones who'd be called upon to provide the firepower if this thing broke into a real little shooting war. They brought up the rear. There was no plan yet for any frontal attack. They were in reserve, just in case. They also had to be ready to move to whichever side of the castle yard they were needed in.

They simply didn't know if they would have to call in that kind of strike. Rosie played back what they knew:

This guy Vieira had hired a surprising number of mercs. He'd tried for the best of the Portuguese, the ones they had with them right now. But that hadn't worked. There hadn't been enough specifics and the men didn't trust the old guy. They thought he was more than a little off his kilter.

He'd ended up with some veterans of the Portuguese Army, not just the seasoned troops from the colonial wars. There had been some others as well: Rhodesians and some men who'd seen action in what had been the Belgian Congo as well as just roustabout mercs who were looking for a fight. They had to assume, then, that the castle was well guarded.

The history of this guy, Vieira, and the missing components that made up the raw materials for the atomic weapons, along with the way that the spies had all been taken out, meant that there was something going on here. There was a lot of smoke that could just mean there was an awfully hot fire taking place.

They only wanted to get inside the old castle and see what kind of fuel Vieira was using to create all this pollution. Maybe he was just getting senile and was deluding himself with new and even more grand images of greatness. Or perhaps he was just getting even more paranoid about the attacks he was sure the Jews were going to make on the national integrity of Portugal. Maybe the recent election of a Socialist president had convinced him that it was all over for Portugal.

Who knew.

Rosie had watched enough foolishness in the United States never to be surprised by anything that political idiots convinced themselves of. They could dream up enemies where none existed, threats of invasion by people who didn't own boats, you name it. Why should a Portuguese be any more sane than a cracker?

A little look-see inside the castle and they could find some answers. That was what he and Beeker and Filipe were going to do. Just take a nice little walk through the place and find out what was going on.

He wanted to whistle as they started to move up the hill. They were crouched over in the most uncomfortable posture possible for running, but it was one that made it less likely that they'd be spotted. They were going after a stronghold. And even if they thought they were going to just have a nice little walk, it didn't mean those mercs the old coot had hired were ready to carry their parasols for them.

13

It's amazing how vulnerable the human head is. Nature has tried to protect the brain—the all-important organ that makes a person human, with all of its gray cells doing their little synapses and whatever the hell else it is that they do. But such a delicate thing as a brain needs even more protection. Nature can't end all the risks, after all. It has done its part with those hard skull bones. If there are some little details that leave some weak points in the head's defense, well those are the breaks.

And there most certainly are ways to damage a brain. If you do them well enough, you take away the life that the brain is supposed to be controlling.

Rosie tossed his knife in the air just to test its balance. He wasn't playing games. This wasn't the time for carnival tricks. The merc in front of him might be a nice guy, but he was on the wrong side. Rosie liked his knife. He thought that the brass thing on the end was a nice touch. It could do a number on that skull. He decided he'd test it.

He moved up on the guy stealthily. The guard was staring off into the distance, as though he was thinking about whatever there was on the other side of the horizon. It was too bad. Because that meant he wasn't paying attention to what was right here. Right here was Roosevelt Boone and a particularly deadly bludgeon on the end of . . .

There was hardly any sound. Just a bit, sort of like the cracking of an eggshell. But it was the sound of a move just as decisive as breaking an egg. Because when you do that, you end the hopes of the little embryo inside. The hard blow that Rosie'd delivered to the merc was just like that. There weren't any more cells doing synapsis dances anymore. The little electric connections that had let the man think and dream and move his muscles didn't exist.

He simply fell onto the ground. There was more noise from his soft landing on the stone walkway than there had been from the mortal blow to his skull. Rosie would remember that. He was lucky this time. The sounds hadn't alerted anyone. But there'd been a lesson learned.

They were moving up onto the ancient battlement that surrounded the castle. Not even Vieira could make believe that the walls provided any real protection these days, so he'd allowed them to fall into a genteel disrepair. The three point men hadn't had any trouble climbing up to the walkway on the top of the walls.

Their only real problem was the discovery of guards. The moon cast surprisingly dark shadows. Its rays were so bright tonight that there was actually some protection in those places where the walls blocked them. Rosie was moving quickly and effectively up his end of the area. He was trusting Beeker to be doing his share at the other. He always had and he always would.

There was one more here to be taken care of. Rosie had pulled the dead merc into his hiding place just in time to avoid letting the new guard see that he was alone now. Rosie waited in the darkness, hoping that the sentry's path would bring him close enough that he could take him out even more silently than the other one had gone.

He still had the brain's vulnerability to work with. The man was going to come close enough. Good. Rosie carefully replaced his knife and got ready. He lifted his hands up in the air in preparation.

Think about popping a big balloon.

That's exactly what he was going to do. But in reverse. The guard came closer . . . Just a few more feet . . . Rosie jumped up and slammed his two hands against the side of the man's head. There was a moment when the merc was utterly paralyzed. Every muscle in his body went taut with excruciating pain.

Rosie reached around quickly and took hold of the man's throat. He knew more than enough physiology to understand just where the jugular was. He found it and pressed it hard. Then there was a sudden slackness in the weight he was holding, and the quick and distinctive stink of his bowels emptying at the moment of his death filled the night air.

The ears—they were the part of the head that left a man defenseless. If you produced enough air pressure, you could quickly and effectively rupture the drums. Some people could get out a scream. But usually there wasn't enough time. Usually you didn't bother with sound when the most delicate and sensitive nerves in your body were screeching with their own special agony. You certainly lost all ability to worry about protecting yourself. The blow to the ears—when properly delivered—could sometimes kill a man. Rosie wasn't taking any chances. He had made sure the guy was gone with the strangulation.

At least the most obvious guards were taken care of. Now they could move on to the major attraction.

Billy Leaps Beeker had taken care of his part of the wall just as effectively as Rosie had done his own. Now, cradling his M-16,

Beak was able to look over the interior and see what the rest of the layout was like.

Just as Filipe had said, there was a huge plaza in the center of the walled area. The actual castle took up only about half the space along three sides. In the center was the open area, which was squared off by the wall.

Beeker wondered later on what he had expected to find. Perhaps he was anticipating scenes of mad scientists working with exotic laboratory equipment. That, or maybe he was counting on some kind of malevolent display that would have convinced him of the evil of the place and the people here. It was always nice to know that your enemy is a son of a bitch. It made it easier to get him.

Maybe he was even bargaining on having the bombs laid out for him. He didn't even know what they would look like. Delilah had explained that they could be very small. Depending on how they constructed them, they could be almost any shape he could imagine. The main thing was that the radioactive material in them wasn't going to be all that dangerous. Until it was activated with all the physics stuff she'd gone through, it wouldn't be hazardous. It would be like walking into a room full of radium watches, that's all, or having a few too many X-rays taken of your teeth.

But there was nothing in the courtyard that filled Beeker's presumptions. Instead, he was looking down on a party.

The women were good-looking and they were dressed in some good clothes. They were circulating easily, so much so that Beeker assumed that none of them were attached to the men who were gathered here. They were hired help, probably. Expensive whores who thought they were in the big time by getting to mingle with international figures.

There was no doubt that the party was cosmopolitan. Beeker

could tell that from the males' clothing. There were some in European suits and others in Western uniforms. But there were more in various forms of native dress.

Billy Leaps saw at least one man who was wearing a uniform similar to al-Kaldi's. Another had the distinctive headgear of a Sikh covering his head. There was one man who was in the traditional dress of a Filipino. He couldn't tell about the blacks. They might have been Africans in their normal clothing or else American blacks were affecting the costumes of that continent.

There was only one thing about them that made sense to Beeker. They were the representatives of the nations with the most vicious and the best-organized terrorist organizations in the world. It was a summit of horror.

It was a crazy reverse image of some of the parties that Delilah had made him attend in Washington, where all the diplomatic assholes made believe that they were cultured and that their behavior at cocktails was more important than the number of innocent people their regimes were murdering back home. They were the same fools who served obscenely expensive caviar while their nationals were begging for powdered milk, rotten grain, anything that might mean that starvation could be staved off for at least one more day.

These were the butchers of the globe. They were the ones who thought that a Christmas party was a bomb exploding in a London department store, that a resort needed a ship hijacked from its port to be noticed by the press, that men in wheelchairs were appropriate targets for fighters for national liberation. But they were acting as though they were standing there and waiting for the queen mother herself to attend the party.

Just then he heard a sound off to his right. He stiffened. He moved quietly and took the knife out, ready to use it if he didn't recognize the cause right away. There was enough moonlight that he didn't have to try to take Filipe out. The Portuguese man was moving quickly, crablike, along the floor of the walkway toward him.

Filipe took a position where he could have as good a vantage point as Beeker. They felt secure enough to have a whispered conversation.

"What the hell is it?" Beeker asked.

Filipe shrugged at first. "Do you recognize any of them?"

"Not individually, but I can guess who they are."

"That one—the one in the African dress over there—is a leader of UNITA, the Angolan group. They're an organization that takes money from Gulf Oil to pay their Chinese-trained soldiers to fight the Cubans."

Beeker didn't even try to follow the logic in all that.

"I know another one. The Sikh, over there. There were rumors that he was the one who directed the assassination of the Indian Prime Minister. Friend Beeker, you've gotten us invited to quite a convention."

"We have to figure out what's going on. Why are there so many?"

Filipe studied the group some more. "If you take their national characteristics and the identities of those I know, there are at least twenty groups represented down there. But you said there were only five bombs?"

"Right, that's what they told me." *And Delilah wouldn't lie about it.*

"Then we have to have a closer inspection. We're in for the long count anyway. We've taken out at least six of their guards among us. There's going to be a change sometime tonight." Covilha looked at the nearest corpse. "He's my size, I could get into his uniform—"

"No, it's too risky."

"There's no choice, friend. I'm the only one in this part of the group that can speak Portuguese. There's no other way. One of us has to go in there and be able to understand what's happening."

Beeker didn't like it. He knew that they were all signed up to take the biggest chances there were. But he didn't understand what was going on down there and he didn't want to let Filipe go. Intelligence was the strongest tool of the warrior. He'd learned that over and over again in all of his experiences. That's why he understood Delilah's concern about the loss of the agents. If you don't know what's waiting for you, you can't be prepared.

But sometimes you just had to go with it. Sometimes you didn't have the choice. He didn't say a word to Filipe. He just turned around and began to unlace the boots of the dead guard.

14

Beeker waited.

He and Rosie had gotten off the wall and had gone back down the hill. They had gathered up the other men and all of them were grouped together silently. They wouldn't move until Filipe came back with the information they needed.

The collection of characters that he'd seen in the courtyard convinced him that this was the place where the action was. He wondered how this guy Vieira had managed to get all of them together without . . .

That was it. He collapsed back against the trunk of the olive tree. Getting the elements for the bombs into Portugal wouldn't have been the problem. That was the easy part. Delilah had explained how small the various pieces were. But these men who were having their little nighttime meeting were something else.

Their pictures would be known to every agent of any standing in the world. There were people in there who the Americans were dying to get their hands on and others that the Russians would like to chat with themselves. They couldn't enter Portugal easily—they could barely move anywhere without being spotted.

The agents had to be taken out to make sure they weren't glancing at arrivals at the airports. The men were the objects that had to be smuggled in so carefully, not the components for the bombs.

And why were they here? If there had been the magic number—five—then Beeker would have understood. They had come for delivery. But there were many more than that. This guy Vieira was up to something. The danger of the bombs was great enough, but there was more.

Knowing that didn't make the time pass any easier. The rest of the men picked up on Beeker's discomfort and stifled any desire for conversation. They'd just have to wait. Biding time was the constant fate of the warrior. They were all used to it.

Cowboy watched the sun rising over the Trás-os-Montes. It was pretty, especially through the colored lenses he was wearing. He was bored, so bored he thought he could scream. There was no end to this. They'd been sitting out of sight of the castle since before midnight and there was no sign of Filipe.

He looked over at Beeker's stony face and knew that the leader was getting worried. They all were. The other Portuguese were hiding it the best. They were just sitting, their eyes scanning the horizon with an attitude close to nonchalance. They were trying to communicate to the Americans that they could trust Filipe. Their own leader had come out of much worse situations in his life and he'd always accomplished whatever task he'd set himself to. Why should this one be different?

Because, Cowboy knew, there was always one that was different. There was always the one that you didn't come back from. It was the way history was written. It was the way things happened to soldiers.

He knew all the stories. A lot of them had come from Nam.

There'd be some guy who'd signed up for extra tours just because he wanted to prove that he could beat the odds. He would, too, until the day before he was supposed to go home. Then, after having survived countless firefights, after having just been missed by a mortar attack, after walking away from the crash of an evacuating helicopter, he'd have a drink too many and step in front of a convoy of ordnance trucks and—bye-bye.

There were always times when you would finally go out on a mission and it just wouldn't work for you. You'd have done something a million times and suddenly, for some unknown reason, you'd make the wrong mistake, often a stupid one. Someone like Marty, who lived with land mines the way normal men lived with their girlfriends' pictures, would step the wrong way—even though he'd never stepped the wrong way in his life before.

There were only so many times that you could test the fates and win. That was all there was to it. There were only so many patrols you could go on and come back. There was a limit to the number of recon gigs you could draw and not find Charlie waiting for you. Filipe had to know that.

He was a pro. After all, it wasn't as though he'd signed up to take dance lessons. He'd agreed to come out with them for a good cause but, just as important, he'd also come out for the action, for that hit of adrenaline that kept men like them alive. There's always the chance you've gambled once too often when you go into the field. That's all there was to it. Cowboy didn't think that this was necessarily the time when Filipe's number was up, not at all. But, who knows?

There was still another possibility. It was dangerous to even think about it. It was a thought that poisoned your mind when you were in the field with a group of men. When you were putting your life on their shoulders, trusting them to be well trained and brave enough to do what they were supposed to do, you had a chance of pulling through. If you started worrying about them, then you got nervous, you lost your timing, you tried to do too much and you did it all too poorly.

There had been times in Nam when there was only one solution to that dilemma. You just had to remove the tumor from the body that was the group of men. If there was someone who was too much of a jerk or who was threatening your life with his misjudgments, then you had to perform a painful operation and remove him.

When the press wrote about "fragging" in Nam they thought it was really a series of personal vendettas. They thought that had to be the reason for the strange—to them—occurrences where American troops would take out one of their own. They just didn't understand.

It wasn't something new to the field in Vietnam. Far from it. It had been going on wherever there was an army in the field. And it wasn't some petty personal stuff being avenged, either. Instead, it was that painful operation.

Who got fragged? The green loot who would order in air strikes and not do his math right so the bombs landed in the wrong place and got his own troops instead of Charlie. Or the officer who was a drunk and who, in the middle of his hallucinations, would demand that a patrol do something suicidal. Or else it would be the asshole who wanted the girl one of his men was planking. Instead of taking the guy on man-to-man, he'd make him pull point duty over and over again. That got to the sense of fair play on the rest of them. It created conflict and it caused unnecessary anxiety, the kind that put the men on edge and could lead them to make mistakes. That was a dangerous tumor, one that had to be gotten rid of.

And it was, with surgical cleanliness when the sickness stood in the wrong place with his back to the wrong soldier. Then there'd be a bullet and the operation would be a success. Because the tumor would have been removed—permanently.

You didn't want to think about distrusting your allies because it created a tumor like that. He glanced again at the group of Portuguese: Tomas, Góis, and Luís were still cool. They weren't men that he'd have to take out.

But they were all just going on gut instinct. What if one of them had wanted to get rid of Filipe for some reason? What if one of them had decided to do a little secondhand fragging on the leader? It'd be easy enough to go on a mission and find a way to finger him.

There was too much loyalty among them, though. Cowboy thought long and hard to convince himself of that. There was too much that passed among the Portuguese that was too much like the stuff that went among the Black Berets. There wasn't any conflict that would divide them, he was sure of it.

There was also the other unthinkable possibility. There were so many mercs who were purely and simply greedy. They wanted more and more of their pieces of silver. Filipe had turned down an offer from this guy in the castle. Maybe he'd hurt the man's feelings. Maybe that made this man put a price on Filipe's head. Would one of these three men be willing to turn in their leader just for some money?

Tomas had told Cowboy a story while they were sitting around earlier. There had been a great Portuguese leader who had fought off the Romans for years. He was the one general the great legionnaires couldn't get. He alone stood on the Iberian Peninsula and kept his part of it free from imperial rule.

There seemed to be something charmed about the guy. There was something that made it seem as though he was that impossible warrior who could go out countless times and not have his number come up. The Portuguese began to revere him. They made him into a symbol of everything that was good in their people and everything that was noble.

Cowboy suddenly hated that story. He looked around at the rest of the Black Berets, all of whom he trusted like brothers, and then he looked at the remaining three Portuguese veterans and he worried. He loathed worrying about them. But that story . . .

The guy's name had been Viriathus. That's what Tomas had called him. The Romans knew the way around valor and strength. They went to the man's most trusted allies and they bribed them to turn the hero over to them. For a little bit of money and a lifetime's worth of guilt, they'd done it. The Portuguese resistance was dead, over with.

There's always a way to get a guy. There's always some reason why he might not come back after an assignment. This could be Filipe's turn. That's all there was to it. No matter how you cut it, no matter what you thought about, he might not be coming back from this one.

There was some movement nearby. They all went on immediate alert. As soon as Cowboy saw Harry's big body approaching them, he relaxed. The Greek had been watching the road, making sure they knew what came in and out of the castle.

"Got a car entering." Harry spoke as laconically as if he were talking about the brand of cat food he'd picked up in the supermarket. "Red sports job, one of those Italian numbers."

"Probably a Lancia," Cowboy muttered. He pulled his beret down over the front of his shades and wondered if he couldn't get some shut-eye.

Then he bolted straight up. "*Beatriz!*" They all looked at him, puzzled. "My lady from Oporto."

"Cowboy, I told you to keep your pecker in your pants.

Jesus, what are you doing thinking about her now? We have a good man in there and we don't—"

"That was her car, Beeker. I'm sure of it. There's no doubt. She said she had an uncle who lived outside the city. The last name didn't register. It was out of context so it didn't make an impression. I just kept her phone number and address. But it's something like this guy's. I'm sure of it. She talked about her long drive, she talked about his trying to get the glory of Portugal back from whoever took it—"

"That's Vieira," Góis said. "That's his thing, recovering the past for the fatherland."

They all stood around wondering what they could or should do with this sudden information. They'd already put Filipe inside the castle. He hadn't returned. Not one of them knew what it meant. But it could be a lot of trouble. Now there was another one with a potential entrée inside the walls.

Beeker thought it over. It involved a lot of risk. But he thought it might be more than worth it. It was a heavy weight to be standing here wondering what had happened to Filipe. This was the most onerous duty of any commander, to wonder if he'd finally sent a man on his last mission. There could be even more risk involved in putting a second man inside the enemy lines. He knew that. But the odds were better in some other ways. And this time they could plan the operation much more carefully.

Beeker looked around the small troop he had at his disposal. These were the best soldiers he'd ever have. There was no reason to question that. They could take care of whatever was going on in there. They just had to understand the objectives better.

"Cowboy, I think you better take a bath in that stream down there. You better look awfully pretty for your lady this morning."

15

Cowboy stood at the entryway to the castle and watched Beatriz walk toward him. She pulled the same number that women had gone through for centuries. She was striding across the courtyard with the haughty air of the lady of the house at first. Then she saw him and her face lit up with all the warmth and all the want that a female can have. Just as predictably, she tried to cover it up. She was trying to drown the memories of their lovemaking and resurrect the humiliation she'd felt when he stood her up.

"*You!*" She did it better than most. There was an edge to her voice and a real bite of anger there. Beatriz wasn't all that young anymore. She was over thirty and still unmarried. That meant there had been many times when a man had hurt her and the accumulation of those memories made every new cut create even greater pain.

But Cowboy smiled his smile and his eyes were still behind those sunglasses that forced her to project her own fantasies onto them. She couldn't resist.

Few of them had been able to. It was one of the many secrets of all those trips to the altar that Cowboy had made. Ladies

127

just didn't know how to say no to him. Part of it was his little boy–like demeanor, some of it came from his blond good looks, but most of it was their memories of how he treated them between the covers.

"Oh, my Cowboy." That was the breaking point. She moved more closely to him and reached out a hand to touch him. But her sense of duty came back. "What are you doing here? Uncle Alfonso doesn't allow—"

He held out the handsome bouquet of wildflowers that he'd picked down on the slopes of the hill before he'd come up to the castle. "They're not much . . ."

It was a killer line to use on a woman. So few men these days were willing to go through the motions of romance that females lived for. To have a male perform them and at the same time be able to make it seem like an inadequate gesture was a combination that few of them had a chance to experience these days, and even fewer women could defend themselves against it.

Beatriz's defenses were gone. She grabbed for the flowers and held them to her nose, smelling them deeply and obviously adoring them as much as if they were the finest roses from the most exclusive shop in Paris. "My Cowboy . . ."

"I couldn't wait to see you again. I was so sorry that I wasn't able—"

"You were so mean to me," she pouted.

"You know I did it only because of something so important that it couldn't wait. I'm so sorry."

"But how am I going to explain you to Uncle Alfonso?" she wondered out loud. "He forbids casual visitors."

"Are you calling me 'casual'?" Cowboy said, trying to remember just the way he used to ask his mama if she really meant he wasn't her favorite in the whole world.

"Of course not." Beatriz was horrified that he'd even think such a thing. "But we must think of a way, he'll be very angry. I know!"

Cowboy just knew she did. He almost said the words for her.

"I'll say we're engaged!"

Bingo!

It was unfair of him, and someplace in his belly Cowboy knew he was feeling badly for pulling that on her. But this was war, baby, and they needed all the weapons they had at their disposal.

Beatriz had been trying to keep herself together in front of the armed guards that were flanking them. She was as worried about their seeing her be too familiar with this *americano* as she was about her uncle.

Then she pulled herself together. "Uncle Alfonso can't object to my fiancé coming to meet him. That would only be proper. He insists on propriety at all times. You'll simply have to act the part well." She smiled. She loved that idea.

"Come, he's in his office now attending to business. This is as good a time as any to introduce you. I am supposed to stay this evening and be hostess for a party he's having for some business associates."

That's a good enough time for them, I suppose, Cowboy thought.

"I already have my room—it's so romantic! We'll have to sneak you into it later." She was whispering now to keep the guards from hearing. "To have you there with me, Cowboy, will be a dream coming true."

He really did have to learn how to feel more guilty when he did these things. But he'd been with Beeker for too long. Right now he could only calculate that he'd met his objective and was ready to move into the next phase. He had to find out what had happened to Filipe and then alert the rest of the squad, which was still waiting out in the olive grove.

Beatriz took him by the hand and led him through the old castle grounds. Alfonso Vieira was sitting in a chaise lounge drinking from a tall, iced glass. He beamed at his niece, on whom he obviously doted. But his expression came within inches of being rude when he turned to Cowboy after Beatriz had given him the good news in a whispered family conference.

"My darling girl has informed me that you are to be married." There wasn't just anger in Vieira's voice. There was disbelief as well. Cowboy recognized it from other men whose women he'd wanted to marry. There was almost an air of relief in it. If Beatriz was really finally going to be taken to the altar, the guy would be jubilant. He just had to have proof.

Cowboy supposed he didn't look like the most desirable suitor to Vieira. He had been lucky to wear the same size clothing as Tomas, who'd had some civilian stuff with him. But as he stood there, with his blond hair and his sunglasses, he realized he must look like a hick American tourist.

He was wearing loose pants, not unlike some peasant dress that he'd seen around the city. The shirt was brightly embroidered and made of homespun linen. He had on a pair of rough Portuguese open-toed sandals. He did not look the part of an elegant groom-to-be.

Beatriz saved the day on that count. "Isn't it wonderful that an *americano* has decided to wear national dress."

Since Vieira's suit was obviously tailored, and just possibly by someone on Savile Row, Cowboy wasn't sure just how much he would approve of the flyer's wardrobe. But her remark had thrown him off. It was amazing what a woman could see, when she tried hard enough, to convince herself that the man she loved was a hero.

Cowboy didn't want to lose the advantage and he didn't want to let Vieira get back to the original impression. He'd had enough experience with Latin fathers and other men who had women under their care to know their real weakness. If those females had to marry an American, at least make it one who had money.

"Senhor Vieira, it certainly is a pleasure. Why, I just love this little house you have here. It reminds me of my daddy's place back in Dallas."

Vieira, obviously more used to people being awed by his castle, was taken aback. It was seldom that anyone would think to compare this place to their own abode. And *Dallas!* To the foreign mind, that could only mean great wealth.

"It is a pleasure to have you here, Mr. Hatcher," Vieira said. But he still wasn't convinced. The great worry of Latin men was that these Americans who did have money were playboys who would squander it and leave their wives penniless. Or, worse, would come to the woman's relatives and expect to be bailed out. It was important to convince them that he had his own source of income, at least a well-paying job.

"Yup, never looked inside one of these European jobs, though. I'm usually too far up there to take a look-see." He pointed to the sky. "Pilot," he explained simply. "I ferry those 747s back and forth for Delta."

Cowboy could see Vieira relax now. An American pilot earned decent money. Even if there was only a little bit from the family to supplement it, a woman could do very well to be married to such a man.

The conversation became much more friendly after that. Cowboy heaped on the good-ole-boy stuff and was happy to sit there and fulfill the fantasies of both Beatriz and her uncle. He might look like a clown to the old man, but he was a possible savior. Who knew how many men had almost taken the woman off his hands? And to have his family's women taken care of was of obvious importance to the old guy.

"You are Catholic, aren't you?" The way that Vieira asked the question told Cowboy what the preferred answer was.

"Sure am. My sainted mother made sure that all of us went to church schools. I learned under the strict discipline of the Sisters of the Bloody Martyr."

"There is no substitute for religious discipline in a young life," Vieira said. He obviously meant it as well.

"Couldn't agree with you more, Alfonso. I wouldn't be the man I am today if I hadn't had it."

Cowboy didn't like this turn of the conversation. There were definite limits to his ability to carry off this part of the deception. He was pleased that Vieira went onto automatic pilot and talked nonstop about the degradation of the Church at the hand of the reformers. The way he described it, Vieira was still pissed off at Martin Luther. He hadn't even worked his way up to the current century when a guard came and interrupted him with a whispered message.

"Of course," the man said. He stood up and offered his hand to Cowboy. "Mr. Hatcher, it has been a pleasure. I haven't had such an opportunity to have such a conversation in quite a while. It is good to hear the views of the younger generation on these subjects and to know that they are not all in favor of guitar-playing priests who want to be revolutionaries.

"I'm afraid I must go now. There is some pressing business." He frowned. "You must excuse me, but there is a very important meeting here tonight. Of course you are welcome to the hospitality of my house. But I am afraid that I will have to dine with my other guests and—since the meeting is quite confidential—I must beg you to take your own meal this evening in your rooms."

"Uncle Alfonso!" Beatriz didn't like this turn of events at all.

"My dear, I know it sounds too rude, but there's no option. I do trust Mr. Hatcher to be a gentleman in all ways. If there is a chaperone, I would understand that you would rather dine with him rather than with my guests and I excuse you from your obligations as hostess."

"Maria will be happy to sit with us."

Her real goal achieved, Beatriz grabbed Cowboy's arm and led him away.

"Sorry, honey. But there's just no other way."

Beatriz looked at him with imploring eyes. There had been one moment when there had been a mixture of fear and excitement, when she thought that he was only playing some kind of decadent American sex game on her. But now it was clear that her beloved Cowboy had other ideas that had nothing to do with their courtship.

He was putting the final touches on the knots that held her tightly to the bedposts. He'd taken her skirt and ripped it into long pieces, not only to bind her, but also to create a gag that kept her from yelling out and alerting the guards.

He had no idea just what Beatriz had said to the old maid who was supposed to be their chaperone. But he was sure the orders included her disappearing for a long time. Beatriz hadn't given any indication that this was going to be a quickie night.

There was a lot of work to do in the castle and the sooner he got to it the better. He gave her a peck on the cheek and remembered, fondly, the way she'd cried out those fado songs the first night they met. He'd treasure them always. It was a little solace that she'd be able to sing them with even more conviction when she had the memory of his betrayal.

"Too bad, Bea, honey. You would have looked dynamite in white."

16

Cowboy needed to be armed. He'd come into the castle cold. They didn't want to take any chances, especially since the borrowed clothing hadn't given him many opportunities for hiding any substantial weapon well.

There were plenty of guards around the place. He'd seen at least a dozen different men in the short while he'd been here. Other people might think they were a danger; to him they were simply a walking salvage yard right now. He wasn't trying to avoid them. He was trying to find one.

He was sure that the word had gone out in the barracks that Senhorita Beatriz had a gentleman caller. They were probably under orders to treat him with kid gloves. That was good. It meant that they wouldn't be on any kind of alert if they saw him. At most they'd want to usher him quietly and politely back to his room.

"*Senhor!*" Cowboy stopped short when he heard the challenge. He turned and saw a man not much larger than himself come down the corridor toward him. The guy threw out a string of Portuguese words that Cowboy could honestly indicate he didn't understand.

The guard tried to use some hand signs to convince the flyer to go back toward his room. They certainly weren't anxious for him to see much of the sights in this place, at least not tonight. *Just whets my appetite*, Cowboy thought to himself.

He was smiling blankly as the man kept up trying to pantomime his directions. Then, when he felt the man had been put through enough of this foolishness, Cowboy simply took a hand and chopped it viciously against the guy's windpipe. It was a particularly effective little move that they practiced all the time. Not only did it make sure the enemy would be dead in a quick moment, but the hard side of the palm smashing against the larynx made sure he couldn't utter a sound of any kind while he was still living.

The Portuguese rolled his eyes back into his head. A hand dropped his rifle as he began his last drop to the floor. Cowboy knew the man was beyond caring whether or not his skull hit the stone surface and he didn't bother breaking his fall. He was much more interested in the semiautomatic. He grabbed for it just in time.

He knew about this one. It was unusual for them not to have at least tried out every major rifle on the market, but the Belgian arm had just come out recently. It was an FNC Assault Rifle. Great little toy, it had gotten the best reviews, including procurement by the Swedish Army, which had some of the highest standards in the world.

This particular model was able to take M-16 magazines. The manufacturer was hoping for some sales to NATO countries and knew the rifle would have to take that standard issue. It wasn't only a decent weapon, it was one of the most accurate being made, at least according to reputation. This was something that a marksman like Cowboy could use to full advantage. There was a thirty-rounder of 5.56 hardball in it right now.

That should more than do it. Cowboy especially appreciated the bayonet mounted on the barrel. He had a feeling that was going to come in handy.

He clutched the gun with more passion than he had embraced Beatriz tonight. He loved the weapon even more, he had to admit it. Walking through these hallways without something substantial in his hands hadn't been a pleasant experience.

His first objective was to find Filipe. There was a chance that the guy wasn't alive. He knew that. But if he was, then he knew more about what was going on than Cowboy could ever discover himself.

It was a big castle and he was barely oriented to its size and its passageways. But he had to look for the man. He assumed that the wing he was in now was for the family. He knew that Vieira's own quarters were nearby, Beatriz had mentioned that. The formal rooms he'd been walking through were in the central part of the castle. The guests were housed in the opposite wing. Cowboy sincerely doubted that Filipe was being considered a guest right about now.

That left the basement. This place was old enough that there might actually be one of those ancient dungeons in it. It was worth a little tour to find out.

Cowboy wasn't interested in appearing to be casual anymore. He moved through the castle very carefully. He didn't come across many guards. They wouldn't be worried about the family wing, for one thing, and whatever little social event Vieira had going on was something that would attract much more of their attention.

He walked down the ancient stairway toward the cellar. He just missed walking in on one group of mercs who were sitting near the kitchen playing cards. A radio and their loud laughter were the only things that warned him.

Beeker was right. Goddamnit, the miserable Marine bastard was absolutely right about maintaining vigilance at all times when they were in the field. Cowboy could listen to the men as they talked in English to one another. He knew from their accents that they were Rhodesians.

That was a dangerous group of men to run up against. The Rhodesians were that special category that had always attracted the employers of guns-for-hire. It was the favorite category of the French Foreign Legion, for one. They just loved taking on men who had no country left. When a man's own nation was simply erased from the globe, he was the one who was willing to sell his military skills to the highest bidder without a thought.

Men like the Black Berets and the Portuguese colonial soldiers still had a claim to their homeland. They could still at least dream that they were the ones who understood what national honor was all about, and they could at least fantasize that the trends in their countrymen's thoughts would change and give them back a place of pride.

But when you'd grown up in a white world in Africa called Rhodesia and your childhood memories were all about playing cricket and having tea with your mother, then you turned around and suddenly that same place was black Zimbabwe . . . well, you acquired a unique form of bitterness about the world then. You had few things that you could count on. After all, if your native land could be removed from the world, what could you be secure about? Why believe in anything? For a fighting man that had to be a trauma something like watching your mother die.

These Rhodesian mercs were some of the best. But they weren't playing by Beeker's rules, and that meant they were at risk. They had given up their advantage by coming together when they were supposed to be spread about the castle wing. They figured everything was under control in this part of the building and that they'd have plenty of warning from the outer rings of protection if there was some danger.

Billy Leaps would have eaten them for breakfast if he had discovered that his men had committed the sin of underestimating an enemy.

Lucky for them, Cowboy could go right around their group and down the next flight of stairs without moving into their field of vision. He wouldn't have wanted to chance the sounds of a burst of automatic rifle fire. But he'd have done it if that was the only way to go.

The bottom stairway marked more than a passage underground. The castle had been renovated to some extent. There were electric lights and running water. But the improvements didn't extend this far.

The illumination here was from blazing torches. It made Cowboy feel creepy, as though he'd walked into a horror movie. The stone walls weren't as smooth. They obviously weren't worried about the reactions of fashion-conscious visitors to the decor down here.

The torches threw spectacular, moving shadows against the walls. That freaked Cowboy a bit. He had to pay particular attention to the possibility that his moves were obvious to anyone who was alert, even at a great distance and around corners.

He did his best to duck and maneuver so the flames didn't project too much of an image of his body. He was pretty sure he was successful.

He knew it when he came to the first armed merc. He was standing in the hallway smoking a cigarette. He was just as lax as the jokers upstairs. His rifle was against the wall across from him. He wasn't going to be able to reach it.

Cowboy stood about six feet away from him. He gauged how long it would take him to make the move. He weighed the

FNC in his hands and looked once more at the bayonet at its tip. He thought it looked beautiful.

Cowboy prepared himself. He remembered all of his conditioning and training at that one moment. He gripped the butt of the rifle so tight that, without even looking, he knew his knuckles were turning white.

He moved quickly, careful that his sandaled feet glided over the floor softly. The guard was looking in the other direction, not at anything in particular, just passing the time while he smoked his cigarette and waited for his relief.

He heard something. Still relaxed and showing no indication of any kind of alarm, he turned toward Cowboy. There was a smile on his face. In that split second Cowboy thought the man must have been expecting someone to come and give him a chance to get a cup of coffee or go to the crapper.

It was a bad assumption on the guard's part.

There was a slight *Ooompf!* as the hardened steel bayonet slipped into his belly. It was from disbelief as much as anything else. The pain didn't have time to register. Cowboy was going to do the man a favor and keep him from ever having to experience it.

He knew the bayonet cut itself wasn't enough to do the man in, at least not right away. It could take a long while for the bleeding to get bad enough to make sure the man was out of the way. Cowboy didn't have the leisure to allow that.

He still had a hard hold on the stock. He savagely pulled up on it and felt the man's flesh rip from the force of the cut. There was a moment of terror on the man's face as he realized that he'd just lost his belly. It was spilling onto the floor. But the good part—which he never would be able to appreciate— was that death came more quickly and he didn't have to think about those things very long at all.

The fact that there was a guard here was good news to Cowboy. That meant there was something worth protecting. It could be something valuable or it could be something that Vieira didn't want roaming eyes to see. Whichever, it meant there was something that Cowboy was going to investigate even further.

He stepped over the now lifeless body on the hallway floor and moved to the door on the other side. He put his back against the wall right beside the opening. He reached out and very carefully tested it to see if it was locked. It moved slightly, just enough to reveal a strip of light brighter than that given off by the torches. Cowboy took a chance and moved a bit more so he could look inside.

Filipe!

The surge of relief that Cowboy felt when he saw his new pal was quickly cut off by the circumstances he was witnessing. Covilha was chained with heavy iron shackles. His body bore the marks of intensive interrogation. There were some lines across his chest and belly that were going to turn into scars if Cowboy could ever get him out of this.

There was another man in there who was moving toward the Portuguese veteran now. He spoke with an English accent, but Cowboy didn't think he was Rhodesian. He had a small package in his hands.

"Really, you've proven to be quite a subject." The man was smiling as he talked to Filipe. "You have withstood an abnormal amount of pain. I'm afraid your heroics are misplaced, however. You should know that there are always ways to make even the most valiant man talk.

"I could use some of the more . . . *sophisticated* methods. There are drugs, of course. But my employer hasn't seen fit to provide too many of them. They may be needed for more gracious interviews and opportunities for persuasion than this one.

The setting is so perfect, however, that I think I'll allow it to guide my inspiration."

He held up a small cardboard box. In his other hand he had a simple needle and thread. "I'll explain just what I am going to do, Senhor Covilha. Perhaps if you understand, you could save yourself a very trying experience.

"We need to know precisely what you were doing coming to the castle and we insist on knowing just who sent you. Your purpose was desperate enough that you were willing to kill to get inside. Your story about being suddenly interested in Senhor Vieira's employ is hardly one that justifies such tactics. Now, will you tell me?"

"I've told you all you're going to get."

Cowboy thought the man had balls. He felt a great deal of respect for Filipe right then. Whatever else, the guy wasn't going to give in to this asshole with his toys.

"But I said I'd explain," the Englishman went on quietly. "These are some of the most primitive life forms in the world, senhor. They are commonly called cockroaches. They go any-where and they have survived innumerable natural enemies. It's said that if there were to be a nuclear war, they might be the only life form to live.

"One reason for their heartiness is their willingness to eat anything. Now, this"—he held up the needle and thread—"is my assurance that when I put these interesting little creatures on your eyes, they won't escape. Simply and purely, they'll be trapped by the sutures I intend to make. They might panic, perhaps they'll just be hungry. But whether they are intent on a meal or on escape, they are going to achieve their goal by the simple means of gnawing.

"It is a very painful thing, Covilha. I don't think you want to experience it."

However much Cowboy had admired Filipe before, he couldn't blame the man for suddenly being petrified. He was staring at the little box. He must have been able to see the filthy little beetles running around inside it. He had to be imagining them trapped by his eyelids, chewing, biting, burrowing . . .

The man put the things down on a table and reached into the box to pull out one of them. He held the oversized bug between his fingers and lifted it in front of Filipe to force the Portuguese to see the disgusting cockroach.

"Your choice."

"Not yours, bastard."

The man turned to see who had dared yell at him. He saw Cowboy standing there with the FNC Assault Rifle and its bloodied bayonet. This time, when Cowboy raced across the room with the deadly blade leading the way, he felt no remorse at all. He felt some great primal release as the weapon buried itself into the English neck.

He didn't even care about the flood of blood that escaped from the guy's jugular vein and cascaded down onto the floor, splashing up onto Cowboy's clothes.

All he cared about was killing the man and hoping he could kill the dreams he knew he'd be having about cockroaches chewing their way through his blue eyes for the next few years.

<h1 style="text-align:center">17</h1>

"I'm sorry you ever saw me this way."

"Naked? Hell, Filipe, I've seen plenty of guys bare-butted before. Locker rooms, barracks . . ."

"I don't mean that," Covilha said as he painfully pulled the Englishman's bloodstained pants over his bruised legs. "I mean . . . frightened. I was going to tell him, Cowboy. I was going to give in."

"That's what you say now," Cowboy said, dismissing the idea with a wave of his hand. "But you wouldn't have done it. You would have found that extra reserve of courage at the last minute."

Like hell, Cowboy said to himself. He knew damn well that there are things that a man just can't stand. There were some of the gutsiest gung-ho monsters that ever spent a day in the Marine Corps who'd faint when you showed them a syringe or puke if you threatened to put them in the same room as a snake. Every man has his weakness. He didn't feel any worse about Filipe just because the Portuguese didn't feel so hot about having some cockroaches crawling through his eyeballs.

Maybe it hadn't even been the bugs. Maybe it was the idea of going blind. That could do it to some men, too, knowing that some part of them was going to be taken away. He'd seen honest-to-God heroes fall apart when they lost a limb, and he knew damn well that if someone told him his pair of crown jewels were going to go if he didn't cooperate, well, the odds would change, that was all.

If he ever did question Filipe's courage, the view of the guy moving now took care of that. Just bending over to secure the shoes on his feet was causing enormous pain. There was no way around that.

"Maybe you should just fill me in and let me take care of it. I have a signal to get the rest of them in here."

It was a bad mistake. After having displayed the slightest weakness in front of the flyer, the Portuguese wasn't about to let any other flaw in his military ability show.

"I will do my part."

Damn, he sounded just like a goddamn Marine. Cowboy almost asked him if there was a Portuguese Marine Corps and then stopped himself. He knew there had to be and it would only depress him if he discovered that he'd tripped across still another brand of leatherneck. The American type was more than enough for him to handle, thank you.

Filipe grimaced as he moved about, but the circulation was coming back into his limbs and he was quickly picking up more mobility. There were still angry red marks at his wrists and ankles where the shackles had bitten into his flesh. The bastards had really given it to him. Cowboy looked down at the dead body on the floor and was happy to know he'd taken care of the son of a bitch.

"We have only the one rifle," Filipe finally said, as much to indicate his being ready to move as to point out the obvious.

"We got a walking stockpile upstairs." Cowboy quickly explained how easygoing the guards were. But he was also worried about something else. "They never told me any details about this meeting. I don't know what time it's taking place. It could have been that the mercs knew that the 'guests' were back in their rooms for a period of time. As soon as they're scheduled to come out, there may be tightened security."

"There will be, trust me. I found out some things before I was stupidly captured."

"Filipe, stop running yourself down. So they suckered you. It's happened to all of us. The thing is we got you out and now there's a job to do."

Filipe took the sharp command well. He knew Cowboy was right. This wasn't the time to bemoan past errors.

"There's going to be a sale tonight. An auction. It must be for the bombs. The people who gathered here have been going to meetings with Vieira and some man from Coimbra—a scientist of some sort. I'm not sure exactly what went on, but I'm pretty sure it was a question of explaining the workings of the bombs and how to handle them."

"Auction? You mean this asshole's just going to sell them to the highest bidder? He's so strange he's willing to risk nuclear war just for the bucks?"

"We don't know that. I just overheard discussion about the 'bids.' That must mean money—at least in some way. We have to find out and we have to stop the action."

We have to do even more than that. There's a fortune in bounties on those men out there, Filipe. I think you and your men are going to be able to live a long time without worrying about the size of your military pensions. The Mossad alone would pay a good pile of good money for some of those heads. I think we're going to go hunting, pal. For some very big game.

They moved up the stairway. Cowboy insisted on taking the lead. He was the one who could move the fastest and respond the quickest. They couldn't take the chance that Filipe's bruises would mess up quick reaction time.

They'd compared notes on the layout of the place and agreed that they had to move to the ground level and then into the formal rooms that were in the central wing. Filipe had confirmed Cowboy's guess that the meeting would be held there. The Portuguese had gotten that far in his investigations.

They moved into the hallway after they went through the door. Cowboy was worrying about the look of expectation that the one downstairs had shown. If it was really close to the time for a changing of the guard, then he might be missed and the Englishman might be discovered. The blood that had escaped from both their bodies hadn't wiped clean from the porous stone floor. There was just no way to effectively remove the evidence of the attack in the basement.

The Rhodesians weren't at their radio. That was another bad sign. They probably were at their posts now. The action was taking place and their little rest was over. Filipe and Cowboy looked at one another. They knew the danger level had just increased.

They crept along the corridor, neatly bypassing the kitchen, where peasant women were too busy preparing a feast to notice them. There was another flight of stairs. Filipe gestured that he wanted them to go up them. It made sense to the flyer and, while he clutched his FNC, they softly climbed the steps.

They made it to the top without making much of a noise. There was another guard standing inside a doorway that seemed to open out onto a small balcony hanging over a large formal hall. He was an Asian of some sort. Cowboy vaguely wondered what civil war or deposed regime had given him his training.

It didn't matter all that much. It hadn't been good enough to protect him right now.

He handed Filipe his FNC and moved toward the man. There wasn't time for any fancy stuff and they couldn't take the chance that anyone would see them.

Cowboy felt the sweat building up under his arms. This was one of the moments of truth. He had the sickening feeling there were going to be lots of them tonight. He lurched out and grabbed hold of the man with one fluid motion. One of his hands went to the guy's mouth to instantly gag him and the other wrapped around his neck.

Getting his elbow joint under the man's chin and exerting all the strength he had in his arms, Cowboy jerked the man so hard and quickly that there was hardly any hope for him to fight back.

Filipe had moved just as quickly to wrench the FNC out of the man's hands. The guard was so intent on his own survival that he let the weapon go without much of a battle.

The bastard wouldn't go easy though. He knew his stuff and reacted quickly. He bit the inside of Cowboy's palm hard. The flyer could feel the teeth cutting through his flesh. He had a sharp wave of nausea that almost overwhelmed the pain when he realized that the small Asian man had actually taken off a piece of his flesh. But their only hope was to get him out of the way as quietly as possible. Cowboy stifled all the human instincts in his body that wanted to cry out from the horrible pain and more terrible sensations.

But finally the body in his grip collapsed. There was no more fight left. The elbow joint had done its work and killed him. They moved the corpse out of the way and left it on the hallway floor outside.

Filipe was armed now. There were two of them with the

powerful and accurate FNCs. But they had only one magazine apiece. Cowboy gestured to the fallen body and made sure that Filipe understood that there were no extra rounds available to them. If they started firing, they were going to have to be more careful than they had ever been before in their lives.

Thirty rounds might sound like a lot to a civilian. But both Cowboy and Filipe understood the danger. Cowboy knew that the FNC had different settings. One was for a three-round burst. He simply didn't know the rifle well enough to understand what that setting was. If he pulled the trigger, he might get off three bullets, not just one. There was always the other problem with automatic rifles. If you weren't intimately familiar with the thing, it could easily fire off an even longer burst with only the slightest touch to the trigger.

With these limitations they had to be even more careful and they had to understand even more what was going on down in the hall. They moved on their bellies to avoid being seen by anyone who might glance up to the balcony.

They got out onto the slight protrusion and were able to witness the most dangerous garage sale in history taking place right before their eyes.

Vieira was at the head of a long three-sided table. The others were seated as though they were attending a formal dinner party. Their plates were clean. Obviously the main course had already been finished. They seemed uncomfortable in the straitlaced setting that their host had devised. But whatever he was offering was more than enough to make up for any inconvenience. They were all obviously willing to put up with his demands.

"Gentlemen"—Alfonso Vieira was speaking to the assembled guests—"it is time for you to make your bids. I will go over the ground rules one more time.

"Each of you has deposited a million dollars in gold in a

special account in Zurich." There were at least twenty different groups represented down there. Cowboy was the Black Berets' banker and he suddenly had visions of a lot more money than would ever be needed to take care of the Portuguese friends' retirement.

"That was simply earnest money, so to speak. I am not interested in monetary gain. It paid your admission to this sale, nothing more.

"You have all been invited here because I trusted you to have the fortitude to utilize the devices which I have secured for your potential use. It would do me no good to hand them over to anyone who would have neither the ability nor the willingness to exploit this . . . unique opportunity.

"I have also, of course, limited the participation to some extent. I had no intention of turning these weapons over to atheistic Communists, nor do I mean to see them put into the hands of anyone that would harm Portugal or who is guilty of having participated in Portugal's decline. In fact, any proposal that includes revenge on our enemies will receive special consideration.

"The devices will be given to the highest bidders. They are primitive weapons, but you've been given all the specifications. After the auction tonight there will be one more sweep of intelligence services in Oporto. My forces are all well placed to make sure that all of you will be able to leave unbothered by any obstructions the great powers might present to you.

"And now, understanding all of that, I invite you to proceed. The bids will be made in the order of the drawing you all held earlier. I am the sole judge of them. They will be measured in terms of effectiveness and originality. Do not bother to try to influence me with money. I have told you that I am not interested in that. I am interested in creating the ultimate terrorist acts."

Cowboy and Filipe exchanged puzzled looks. The auction

didn't involve money? There would be consideration for creativity? What the hell was the madman up to?

"The first bid will be heard from the heirs of the sadly departed al-Kaldi. I am assured that Senhor Ben Aben is in a position to take our colleague's place."

A robed Arab stood up and bowed to his host. "The Forces of Allah believe that their role is to create the maximum havoc in the world. Before he was taken away by the Messenger of God, al-Kaldi had charted our strategy to prepare the way for the righteous with a reign of disorder."

Cowboy remembered those horrible words as the Arab leader screamed at them after receiving his death sentence in the Saharan desert.

"There is a major conference of the world's health scientists to be held in Israel in two months. It is not just a question of destroying Tel Aviv—which this bomb would do very well— but we would also be able to remove most of those people who are capable of providing health and survival on a global scale. To eliminate those personages would be to set modern medical science back decades.

"That is our bid."

There was a murmur of approval that went through the hall. They had obviously expected something much less sophisticated from the Palestinian fanatics than this and they weren't above showing their appreciation for the proposal's finesse.

The next man to stand and make a presentation was a Sikh. "We propose to explode our bomb in New Delhi during the coming visit of the President of the United States. The gesture is supposed to cement relations between the two countries. The elimination of the President and of the Indian Prime Minister will not only cause both countries great anguish but may even provoke a confrontation between the superpowers."

Filipe stiffened when he heard that one. Cowboy knew there was something special in it, but he didn't have a clue as to what.

The next man was European-looking. He wore a working-class suit and was obviously uncomfortable in these elegant surroundings. "I speak for the Basque Liberation Front. We propose to place our bomb in the Paris metro. Properly situated, the bomb will not only destroy the subway—with a maximum death toll if done at the right time—but will also strike at the heart of France. Other countries might live without their capitals, but not France without Paris. With the central government destroyed, we can move to create our own country—finally—from the territories occupied by both France and Spain."

On it went. A group from Indonesia—careful to remind the assembly that that country had taken a small piece of Portuguese colonial territory by force not long ago—Timor, one of the last remnants of empire—suggested that a bomb be used during a goodwill visit of an American nuclear naval task force that was scheduled to call on Djakarta.

An American radical group wanted to explode the bomb at the United Nations during its upcoming plenary session. Cowboy was incredulous as he listened to the insanity that poured out of the mouths of these idiots. He remembered again al-Kaldi's threat: *The rule of terror will come.* This was it. The worst he'd ever dreamed of.

Filipe hit his arm hard to draw him back to the present. He nodded vigorously toward the other side of the room. There was a Rhodesian guard staring in their direction. He'd sensed something wrong; perhaps he was looking for the Asian who was supposed to be standing there. Whatever it was, they were in trouble. He was moving—fast—to check it out.

18

Cowboy and Filipe used their elbows, knees, and bellies to move backward out of the small balcony. Cowboy couldn't help but take another look at the dead Asian guard, hoping he'd find a hidden pistol. But there was nothing more.

They looked at one another and knew this was it. They had only the two rifles and the limited number of rounds. Their expressions said it all: *What the fuck are we going to do?*

Cowboy had come in knowing that any gunfire would bring the rest of the men running. He knew that they were out there, just waiting for the signal. They weren't the type who were going to be sleeping on the job. There had been a more civilized set of signals to use if he had the opportunity—an open fire on one of the battlements was one. He could have used a mirror to flash a message to the olive grove as well. But none of those were viable now. Not even the damn rifle fire. They couldn't waste any of their ammunition.

He suddenly wished that Marty Appelbaum were here. As much as he thought the man was an idiot, it would sure be nice to know that he was standing beside him right now with a nice big pile of explosives to take care of all their trouble. But there were no free lunches in this operation, that was for sure.

"Follow me," Filipe whispered. They moved back down the stairs. Cowboy wanted anything, even just a closet, to hide in that might give them a chance to jump that nosy Rhodesian and hope that he wouldn't be smart enough to have told anyone else where he was going.

But Filipe had thought of something else. The crowd in the hall was hard to hear back here. The old heavy wooden doorways were thick and absorbed the sounds well. He was obviously going to play with that.

He moved to the entry to the kitchen. He seemed to stop for just a moment, either to catch his breath or, Cowboy thought more likely, to will his body to ignore the immense pain it must be sensing right now. But it didn't take long. Filipe knew what pressure they were under. The Portuguese suddenly jumped into the kitchen with the FNC held straight in front of him.

"*Silêncio!*" he ordered the peasant women. They jumped backward, but none were going to argue with the large weapon. Fortunately, none of them gave in to their desire to scream.

Filipe gestured them back into a corner. The men were lucky. There was an easy way to handle them. A walk-in refrigerator was there. They herded the trembling women into it and shut the door, a barrier even thicker and better at muffling noise than the other ones in the house. As soon as he was done securing the locks, Filipe turned to Cowboy and smiled.

"*Knives.*" That was all he had to say.

Cowboy went back to the entrance to the hallway. The Rhodesian was taking his time; that was good news. He probably didn't want to disrupt the assembly just on a hunch. Or else he was gathering up some other men just in case; that was bad news.

While Cowboy stood there and studied the situation and

fought the burning pain in his hand, Filipe went running around the room collecting all the blades he could. A large kitchen like this was a gold mine for him. Cowboy had heard Beeker talk about the way Filipe had taken out the attackers in the alley when the two of them had left the bar. If the man could impress the Black Beret chief, he had to be pretty damn good at it.

Cowboy looked lovingly at the already used bayonet tip. That was his own best hope right now. There was the sound of running coming down the hallway. Cowboy ducked to get out of sight. He was able to see the backs of three uniformed guards as they rushed by him and up the stairs. They were going to find the Asian and then all hell was going to break loose.

They had to get more ammunition! They had to get the rest of the troops in here!

Filipe took up a position behind Cowboy. The best part of the knives was their silence. These weren't the well-tempered and carefully balanced fighting weapons that soldiers were used to. It was going to take all of Filipe's skill to overcome the primitiveness of the weapons.

Cowboy felt his stomach tighten. Then he heard the sounds of angry voices from up the stairs. The gig was up. They were going to be coming down. There was some noise from the hall as well. Some of the bidders must have sensed the danger.

The Rhodesian led the way. He was rushing down the steps with another one of the FNCs in his hands. There were two others who would be behind him. Cowboy sensed Filipe's field of vision and stepped out of the way. This was going to be his show.

There was only the slightest sound of air being sliced apart as the first knife flew. Then there was such a soft sound of metal scraping bone that you never would have heard it if you hadn't been trying to.

The Rhodesian didn't have much choice. Since the blade

went neatly into his forehead, just above the place between his eyes, he wasn't hearing much of anything at all. But he didn't stop his forward motion in time to give his pals any sense of the danger they were in.

The second one got it in the neck. It was a long, thick butcher's knife that was thrown with such force and accuracy that it nearly severed his head from his body. The third one did see that happen. There was no way to shield his vision to keep him from having to watch the way the skull dangled off to one side. But it didn't do much to help him. By the time it had all registered, there was another butcher knife cleaving into his chest and stopping his heart from pumping.

"Let's move," Cowboy yelled. "We have to get up the stairs to a position we can defend. I have to get to a window where I can signal the rest of them."

"Do you know where you want to go?"

"There has to be a room with an outside window in the wing I was in before. We have to chance it. Don't worry about the sounds of gunfire anymore. And now we have the ammunition we need." He reached down and pulled out the magazines from the three dead men's rifles. "Let's move it!"

They raced down the corridors of the old castle. They still weren't sure of the settings of the FNCs, but with the extra rounds they weren't going to spend the time worrying about it.

There was a sudden siren sounding. *God, I hope they hear that!* Cowboy prayed. He wanted the reinforcements to arrive as soon as possible. Even before that!

The alarm had alerted all the armed men in the camp. There were the sounds of footsteps running in all directions it seemed. Even through the heavy doors of the hall Cowboy could hear the angry and frightened voices of the assembly rising up.

They got to another stairway and made their way up it,

taking two steps at a time. There were three uniformed guards running down. They weren't resting this time. The one in the lead saw Cowboy and for the shortest time possible the two of them stared at one another. Then Cowboy's finger moved on the FNC trigger. There was a sudden *Bam-Bam-Bam*.

The guy was dead. The man behind him tripped over his body and went sprawling. When he was in midair there was another *Bam-Bam-Bam* as three rounds went into his exposed belly.

Now they at least knew that the rifles were set to let off triple rounds.

The third man didn't call for a waste of ammunition. He got Cowboy's well-used bayonet in his belly. The pilot used it to throw him over his back. He just lifted the man up as though he were a piece of skewered barbecue and then, using all of his strength, lifted him up and tossed him over his shoulder.

They were clear. They continued their way up. There was a barrage of gunfire when they first turned the last corner. Someone was trying to make damn sure they didn't make this move. They jumped back, listened to some of the wasted warning fire. The noise gave them some bearings on where the attack was coming from.

On a signal they both jumped into the hallway and used their FNCs to deadly advantage. The tumbling .223 slugs roared their mortal messages down the closed-in stonewalled space.

Two guards did a death dance at the other end. Their weapons were thrown from their hands. They were lifted up off the floor by the brutal explosions that were hurled their way. Useless shots, potentially lethal, ricocheted off the stone walls of the castle. But Cowboy and Filipe's luck held. They went toward the dead bodies and the open window they could use to get off a signal to the waiting troops outside.

19

At last!

"Let's go!" Beeker yelled at the men when the siren sounded. They'd been going crazy waiting for a signal from Cowboy. This wasn't one they'd agreed upon, but the wailing was more than enough to justify finally moving.

There were five men armed with M-16s; Marty and Góis carried their M60s. It was miraculous that the two little men could handle the huge weapons. They were so heavy that there shouldn't have been any way for the two runts to lug them up the hill that way, but they did.

The alarm had grabbed all the attention of whatever guards might have been on the walls. Beeker and Rosie remembered the easy way up the battlements that they'd used the other night. They led the force of Black and Purple Berets up the walkway.

As they were just beginning their ascent a fusillade of gunfire erupted inside the castle. It could be Cowboy getting off the final signal; it could be an attack that the pilot and Filipe were launching on their own; it could be the sound of their deaths.

The brutal noise only encouraged the mixed team of Americans and Portuguese. They picked up more speed and rushed up the slope toward the top of the walls.

A guard was unfortunate enough to step in their way. He was obviously shocked to see the team making its assault. But he didn't have time to do anything about it. All the frustration of waiting to know what was happening to their two friends built up. They all unloaded on the poor sucker, making his body into a bleeding piece of Swiss cheese.

They achieved the height of the walls and quickly spread out. Rosie and Tomas sped to the left. They ran into three uniformed guards of some nondescript nationality. Rosie didn't bother to ask for names and addresses, let alone proper identification. He shouldered his rifle and got the first two in the head with a burst of perfectly aimed fire. Tomas took care of the other one with his own little display of marksmanship.

On the other side Harry and Luís were rushing to secure the left flank. They found only one poor slob, a Portuguese, Harry guessed, since he was able to spew out a line of pleas before Luís let him know that they weren't interested in his life story with a burst of automatic fire in his belly.

The actions were causing panic down below. But they were doing something even more interesting and valuable up on the walls. They gave Marty and Góis enough time to set up the M-60s on their pedestals. The automatic rifles, more like cannon with their power and large rounds, were in place for the final chapter in this little story.

The delegates to the auction came running out of the great hall of the castle. Some of them were armed with FNCs and others with handguns. The sounds of the assault had been echoing, bouncing off the huge stone walls of the castle and not giving the insiders any hint as to the location of the danger.

Beeker knew it must have hurt Appelbaum terribly, but the little runt actually did hold back his fire. He must have been crying to open up with his favorite toy. But he understood that strategy demanded that he wait until as many people as possible ran from the doorway.

They were pretty stupid for seasoned military leaders. They would have been better off if they had stayed indoors, under cover. A few of them, Beeker could see, were smarter than the rest. He could make out the barrels of rifles being poked through windows and sweeping the plaza with their sights.

Now, Marty! Beeker silently commanded. As though he had actually heard the words, Appelbaum's M-60 began to sing out its special death aria. Góis began almost as soon as he realized the attack had started in earnest.

The two horrible machines sent choruses of 30-caliber death flying through the courtyard. Their streams of full-copper-jacketed slugs cut down the Sikh as he was still desperately looking around trying to locate the source of the danger. They burst open the skull of the Palestinian who had so recently taken over from al-Kaldi before he could pull the trigger on his FNC and get off a shot at the battlement where he, at least, had momentarily realized the combined Berets forces were. The two SAW gunners would break for only the instant it took to hook up a new belt.

The courtyard became an execution hall for the terrorists. One by one they were mowed down by the relentless fire of the M-60s and the sharpshooting of the rest of the Berets.

There were some who were shooting back now. A sharp *Ping!* beside his wounded ear made sure that Beeker understood that some of the men down there meant business. He pulled back against the battlement walls and got off a quick barrage of rounds that forced his assailant back into the room to escape the sudden rain of deadly broken glass that Beeker's bullets had brought down on the man.

They had the men trapped inside the castle. But that wasn't making Beeker any more comfortable. He couldn't forget that the idiots in there had the makings of five atomic weapons. There was no way to know if they'd been activated yet.

The terrorists were cornered, but that only made them more desperate. This wasn't a group of people who would count on compassion or throw themselves on the mercy of any court in the world. They couldn't. They knew damn well that every system of justice that existed would send them to their execution without a blink of the eye.

Quick thoughts of his immediate destruction swept through Beeker's mind. *At least my son will be safe.* That's the only good thing he could imagine right now. That and the fact that death in an atomic explosion would be so instantaneous and so complete that there wouldn't be a second to think about it and not an ounce of him left to worry about.

Vaporization. That's what they called it when you got it this close to an atomic detonation. You didn't even turn to dust. There wasn't even that much left of you.

They couldn't let themselves be trapped in here by the gunfire coming from the hall. They had to go in and chance whatever might wait for them. To stay here was to give the people inside just the precious minutes they might need to put the bombs together.

Then there was a sudden increase in the fire coming from the hall. But there weren't any rounds being aimed at them! Something was going on inside.

Beeker could hear a series of triple plays in the midst of the confused gunfire. *Bam-Bam-Bam* sounded over and over again, as though whoever was firing the rifles wanted to play a special song to accompany the louder and quicker bursts of the M-60s that Appelbaum and Góis were still setting off to keep the terrorists pinned down.

Bam-Bam-Bam! Slowly but surely the sounds of the three-round bursts became more dominant. Whatever was going on in there, those were the musical notes being played by the winners. Beeker understood the ways these symphonies of death were performed. He only wished that he was sure who the composer was.

Then, suddenly, there was silence. Marty and Góis were swinging their M-60s back and forth on their bipods, just waiting for someone to show his head and give them another excuse to play their deadly songs. But there was nothing at all. The sweat gathered on Beeker's forehead. Fear wasn't something he was used to feeling. But now he wondered if this was the sign that someone in there was getting ready for the final, most complete suicidal act of all, the detonation of the atomic bombs that would remove all trace of them from the face of the earth.

"Hey, Appelbaum! Get your hands off that goddamn cannon. I'm coming out!"

Another wave of emotion surged through Beeker. It was one that he was no more used to than fear: relief. That was Cowboy's voice. They were going to live. They had won one more battle. They could go on and fight another.

He looked down onto the courtyard and saw the flyer and Filipe march out, their arms around one another's shoulders and blood seemingly all over their torn clothes. They weren't very worried about appearances though. It was pretty obvious they were just happy to be alive.

20

They were sprawled out on the Tamariz beach at Estoril. The elegant aristocratic playground was just a fine place as far as Rosie was concerned. It was just fine.

He had a big smile on his face as he watched the pretty Latin ladies doing their promenade thing up and down the beautiful sand. Poor Cowboy was still on his stomach. He'd been that way since they'd first gotten out here. It was his own fault for wearing that skimpy bathing suit. He should have known what a parade of Latin lovelies would do to his physiology and he should have taken some precautions. Like this big baggy pair of trunks that Rosie had on that gave him all the freedom of motion he wanted no matter how enticing the sights might be.

There were some *pretty* things here on the beach. That was for sure. Rosie sipped his tall iced rum drink and thought about a life of this. He could do it. He was sure he could just spend all the rest of his years sitting here and looking at ladies and drinking good rum.

These Portuguese guys were certainly going to have a chance at it. They were on lounges beside Rosie yabbering away in that funny language of theirs. He was sure they were still going about the business of spending the money they'd fallen on.

Even by the time the two groups had split up Vieira's fortune between them they were all left with a bundle that was going to make their lives more than comfortable. The Black Berets already had their fortune well established. They had accounts in banks from Zurich, Switzerland, to Geneva, New York, that Rosie didn't even know the numbers on and he couldn't care less.

All he needed to know was that they had enough for him to go fishing when he got back to the States. He still wanted to spend some time at a cottage on the Gulf Coast. Well, it didn't hurt, of course, that there was enough real folding stuff in his pocket that he could wow one of these ladies with the best meal in town and then take her to the fanciest suite—if she was interested.

He roared with laughter at the silliness of the world. There he was, a street boy from Newark who nearly got the big one in an atomic blast in some Portuguese castle, and all he was really thinking about was his piece of steak and his piece of ass. What a crazy life they led.

Beeker was looking out over the beach from his room in the hotel. There was a knock on the door. He went and answered it.

"Filipe," he said. He put a hand on the Portuguese man's shoulder and gripped it hard with a greeting. "Come in."

The two men took seats and looked at one another. There was some discomfort. Both of them would have been more comfortable out in the field than in this civilized space where there were so many unspoken rules about how they should behave. It seemed as though the two of them were wild tigers that suddenly found themselves in cages side by side.

"It's all done, Beeker," Filipe finally said. "The material for the weapons was picked up by your government people a while ago. I oversaw the transfer. The lady—your lady—"

"She's not mine," Beeker said. There was some truth to it. He didn't own her. But the statement still sounded false in some way. *Maybe I mean I'm hers.*

Filipe shrugged. "She said to tell you she'd see you soon, in Louisiana."

The words seemed to be bad news to Beeker. He stiffened even more and sat up even straighter in his chair. "Why? Did she say why?"

"No." Filipe waited to see if there was anything more the Indian would say. When it was obvious that Billy Leaps had spoken all he was going to, Filipe went on:

"There will be another, different meeting soon. There were so many wanted men in the castle that the agents of the different countries involved got lost in their calculations. They're going to assemble in New York to determine just how much of how many bounties we're going to get. My men like being suddenly rich, Beeker. They thank you."

"They'll get over it," Billy Leaps said. He knew that the Portuguese wouldn't be any more comfortable with a playboy lifestyle than the Black Berets. They might dream about living in luxury and having servants, but they were real fighting men and they'd have to have their fixes of adventure and danger just the way the Americans did. They wouldn't be able to get off the drugs cold turkey any more than the Black Berets.

Filipe wasn't going to argue the point now. "Vieira was insane. It's a good thing he died in that battle. He would have blown up the bombs if he had had the chance. It's good fortune that Cowboy and I ran to that suite of rooms of his and accidentally were standing guard over the bombs. They needed only a couple minutes' work to go off."

"There aren't many accidents in this world, Filipe," Beeker said. And he meant it at some profound level. The pair of them had saved them all with the choice of a place to defend.

"He was crazy, Beeker. Vieira honestly believed that if he could get the superpowers to knock each other off by taking the world to the brink of anarchy with terror, he could lead Portugal back to its place as a great country. He had plans for a 'new order' of Portugal. His merchant empire was to be the centerpiece. He thought it would be like the old days when the explorers went out from Lisbon, Oporto, and other places and planted the flag all over the globe.

"He was willing to destroy everything just to risk his dream coming true."

"He isn't the only one, Filipe. He won't be the last."

"I'm afraid you're right. My men have chosen to take your suggestion and let Cowboy handle their finances along with yours. He seems to do it well and we know little about such things."

"You'll be okay with him."

"Beeker. You and the Black Berets have many battles to fight yet. I know it. I can tell it's true. Just understand that you have some friends in a small European country if you need them. They know how to handle a rifle or two."

"Thanks, Filipe. I mean that."

Covilha stood up and offered a hand for Beeker to shake. After they'd finished Beeker looked at Filipe and said, "I'd like to think that I'll never take you up on your offer . . ." But the words hung between them. They knew about this world and they knew he probably would have to.